"I Thought You Wanted A Divorce."

"I do." He secured the lily behind her ear, his knuckles caressing her neck for a second too long to be accidental. "But first I want the honeymoon we never had."

She gasped in surprise, followed by anger…then suspicion. "You're just trying to shock me."

"How do you know I'm not serious?" His blue eyes burned with unmistakable, unsettling— irresistible?—desire.

She'd barely survived their last encounter with her heart intact. No way in hell was she dipping her toes into those fiery waters again. "You can't really believe I'll just crawl into bed with you."

"Why not? It isn't like we haven't already slept together."

Not that they'd slept much. "That night was a mistake." One with heartbreaking consequences.

Dear Reader,

Wow, I can hardly believe it's already time to introduce you to the last Landis brother! What a delightful journey it has been for me sharing the stories of Matthew, Sebastian and Kyle Landis. Now in *The Tycoon Takes a Wife,* we learn what really happened to Jonah when he traveled to Europe. If you're new to THE LANDIS BROTHERS, no worries! I've penned the tale so you can dive right into this delicious family packed with powerful men.

I do so enjoy connected stories, especially family sagas, so it came as no surprise to me when my interest was piqued by the royal family of Jonah's wife, Eloisa. Stay tuned for more on those intriguing Medina monarchs later this year.

And meanwhile, I'm thrilled to be taking part in Silhouette Desire's exciting A SUMMER FOR SCANDAL continuity miniseries! Look for my "scandalous" contribution to land on shelves this August.

Thank you again for all your e-mails and letters about THE LANDIS BROTHERS as well as my other books! I love hearing from readers, so please feel free to contact me through my new Web site, www.catherinemann.com, or write to me at P.O. Box 6065, Navarre, FL 32566.

Happy reading!

Catherine Mann

CATHERINE MANN

THE TYCOON TAKES A WIFE

Silhouette®

Desire

Published by Silhouette Books

America's Publisher of Contemporary Romance

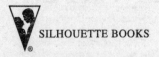 SILHOUETTE BOOKS

ISBN-13: 978-0-373-73026-1

Recycling programs
for this product may
not exist in your area.

THE TYCOON TAKES A WIFE

Copyright © 2010 by Catherine Mann

Books by Catherine Mann

Silhouette Desire

*Under the Millionaire's
  Influence* #1787
*The Executive's Surprise
  Baby* #1837
†*Rich Man's Fake Fiancée* #1878
†*His Expectant Ex* #1895
*Propositioned Into a
  Foreign Affair* #1941
†*Millionaire in Command* #1969
Bossman's Baby Scandal #1988
†*The Tycoon Takes a Wife* #2013

*Wingmen Warriors
†The Landis Brothers

Silhouette Romantic Suspense

Private Maneuvers #1226
Strategic Engagement #1257
Joint Forces #1293
Explosive Alliance #1346
The Captive's Return #1388
Awaken to Danger #1401
Fully Engaged #1440
Holiday Heroes #1487
  "Christmas at His Command"
Out of Uniform #1501

Silhouette Books

*Anything, Anywhere, Anytime

CATHERINE MANN

RITA® Award winner Catherine Mann resides on a sunny Florida beach with her military flyboy husband and their four children. Although after nine moves in twenty years, she hasn't given away her winter gear! With over a million books in print in fifteen countries, she has also celebrated five RITA® Award finals, three Maggie Award of Excellence finals and a Booksellers' Best win. A former theater school director and university teacher, she graduated with a master's degree in theater from UNC-Greensboro and a bachelor's degree in fine arts from the College of Charleston. Catherine enjoys hearing from readers and chatting on her message board—thanks to the wonders of the wireless Internet that allows her to cyber-network with her laptop by the water! To learn more about her work, visit her Web site, www.catherinemann.com, or reach her by snail mail at P.O. Box 6065, Navarre, FL 32566.

To my intrepid traveler and oldest daughter, Haley.
Congrats on taking the world by storm!
You'll always be our princess.

Prologue

Madrid, Spain: One Year Ago

He wanted to drape her in jewels.

Jonah Landis skimmed his fingers along the bare arm of the woman sleeping next to him and imagined which of the family heirlooms would look best with her dark hair. Rubies? Emeralds? Or perhaps even a string of fat freshwater pearls. His knuckles grazed from her shoulder to her collarbone, his five-o'clock shadow having left a light rasp along her creamy flesh.

He usually didn't dip into the family treasure trove. He preferred to live off the money he'd made with his own investments. But for Eloisa, he would make an exception.

Early morning light streaked through the wrought-iron window grilles in the seventeenth-century manor home he'd rented for the summer. A gentle breeze rustled the linen draping over the bed. At first he hadn't even realized she was American, she'd looked so at home walking among the Spanish castle ruins. And exotic. And hot as hell. While she'd picked her way through the scaffolding making notes, he'd lost track of his conversation with fellow investors.

Most labeled him the impulsive one in his family, not that he cared much what others thought of him. Sure he took risks on a regular basis in his work realm and private life, but he always had a plan. And it had always paid off.

So far.

Last night, for the first time, he hadn't planned a damn thing. He'd simply jumped right in with both feet with this coolly intriguing woman. He wasn't sure how the decision would pan out in the long run, but he knew they were going to have one helluva summer.

The rest? They could take a day at a time.

"Uhmmm," she sighed, rolling to her side and draping her arm over his hip. "Did I oversleep?"

Her eyes were still closed but their dark, rich color had cloaked the hauteur of an Ottoman empress. He'd lost plenty of time wondering about the woman behind them during historical reconstruction meetings.

He checked the digital clock resting on a carved walnut end table. "It's only six. We still have a couple of hours before breakfast."

Eloisa burrowed her head deeper in the feather pillow, her black hair fanning a tempting contrast across white cotton. "Am still so sleepy."

She should be. They'd stayed up most of the night having sex…catnapping…showering…and ending up tangled together all over again. It didn't help that they'd had a few drinks.

He'd limited himself to a couple, but those two seemed to hit her harder than him. He stroked back her long black hair, so smooth it glided through his fingers now as it had when she'd been over him, under him.

He throbbed from wanting her all over again when he should be down for the count for a while yet. She needed the rest more.

Jonah eased from the bed, fresh morning air from outside whispering over his skin. "I'll call down and have someone from the kitchen send breakfast up here. If you have any preferences, speak now."

She flipped to her back, eyes still closed as she stretched, her perfectly rounded breasts on amazing display as the comforter slipped to her waist. "Hmmm, anything is fine with me." Her words were slurred with sleep. "I'm having the most wonderful dream—"

Eloisa paused, scrunching her forehead. She peeked through barely open inky lashes. "Jonah?"

"Yeah, that would be me." He stepped into his silk boxers and reached for the phone.

Her gaze darted around his room quickly, orienting. She grasped the comforter and yanked it up, bringing her hand closer to her face. Suddenly she went stock-still and frowned.

"What's the matter?"

She couldn't possibly be shy after last night. It wasn't as if they'd kept the lights off.

"Uh, Jonah?" Her voice squeaked up a notch.

He sank to the edge of the bed and waited, already thinking through at least five different ways he could distract her throughout the summer.

She extended her arm, splaying her fingers wide. Sunshine through the window glinted off the simple gold wedding band he'd placed there last night. Eloisa blinked fast, her eyes going wide with horror.

"Oh my God," she gasped, thumbing the shiny new ring around and around. "What have we done?"

One

"**C**ongratulations to the bride to be, my little princess!"

The toast from the father of the bride drifted from the deck of the paddleboat, carried by the muggy Pensacola breeze to Eloisa Taylor back on the dock. Eloisa sat dipping her aching feet in the Florida Gulf waters, tired to the roots of her ponytail from helping plan her half sister's engagement party. Her stepfather had gone all out for Audrey, far more than a tax collector in a cubicle could afford, but nothing was too good for his "little princess." Still he'd had to settle for a Monday night booking to make the gala affordable.

The echo of clinking glasses mingled with the lap of waves against her feet. Dinner was done, the crowd so well fed no one would miss her. She was good at that, helping people and keeping a low profile.

Putting together this engagement party had been bittersweet, forcing her to think about her own vows. Uncelebrated. Unknown even to her family. Thank God for the quickie divorce that had extracted her from her impulsive midnight marriage almost as fast as she'd entered it.

Usually she managed to smother those recollections, but how could she not think about it now with Audrey's happily-ever-after tossed in her face 24/7? Not to mention the cryptic voice message she'd received this morning with *his* voice. Jonah. Even a year after hearing it last, she still recognized the sexy bass.

Eloisa. It's me. We have to talk.

She swept her wind-whipped ponytail from her face, shivering from the phantom feel of *his* hand stroking her face. A year ago, she'd indulged herself in checking out the heritage of her real father. A summer indulgence had led her to one totally wrong man with a high-profile life that threatened her carefully protected world. Threatened secrets she held close and deep.

Eloisa blinked back the memories of Jonah, too many given how little time she'd spent with him. They were history now since she'd divorced him. Not that their twenty-four-hour marriage counted in her mind. She should ignore the call and block his number. Or at least wait until after her sister's "I do" was in the past before contacting him again.

A fish plopped in the distance, sailboat lines clinking against masts. The rhythmic, familiar sounds soothed her. She soaked up the other sounds of home, greedily gathering every bit of comfort she could find. Emerald-green waters reflected a pregnant moon. Wind rustled through palm trees.

An engine growled softly in the distance.

So much for a late-night solitary moment. She shook dry one foot, then the other and glanced over her shoulder. A limo rolled closer. Late arriving guests? Really late since after-dinner dancing was well underway.

Reaching for her sandals she watched the long black stretch of machine inching beside the waterway. The shape of the sleek vehicle wasn't your average wedding limo. The distinctive grille glinted in the moonlight, advertising the approach of an exclusive Rolls-Royce. Tinted windows sealed off the passengers from view, but left her feeling like a butterfly pinned to the board of a science project. The private area should be safe. Yet, was anywhere totally secure, especially in the dark?

Goose bumps stung along her skin and her mouth went dry. She yanked on her shoes, chiding herself for being silly. But still, Audrey's fiancé was reputed to have some shady connections. Her stepdad could only see power and dollar signs, apparently unconcerned with the crooked path that money took.

Not that any of those questionable contacts had cause to hurt her. All the same, she should return to the floating party barge.

Eloisa jumped to her feet.

The limo sped up.

She swallowed hard, wishing she'd taken a self-defense class along the way to earning her library studies degree.

Okay, no need to go all paranoid. She forced her hands to stay loose and started walking. Only about thirty yards ahead, and she would alert the crew member at the gangway. Then she could lose herself in the crowd of dancers under the strings of white lights. The engine grew louder behind her. Eloisa strode longer, faster.

Each breath felt heavier, the salt in the air stinging her over-sensitive pores. Her low heel caught between planks on the boardwalk. She lurched forward just as the car stopped in front of her.

A back door swung wide—not even waiting for the chauffeur—and blocked her getaway. She couldn't continue ahead, only sideways into the car or into the water. Or she could back up, which would take her farther from the boat. Frantically she searched for help. Would any of those seventy-five potential witnesses in party finery whooping it up to an old Kool and the Gang song notice or hear her?

One black-clad leg swung out of the limo, the rest of the man still hidden. However that Ferragamo python loafer was enough to send her heart skittering. She'd only met one man who favored those, and she hated how she still remembered the look and brand.

She backed away, one plank at a time, assessing the man as he angled out. She hoped, prayed for some sign to let her off the hook. Gray hair? A beer belly?

Anything non-Jonah.

But no such luck. The hard-muscled guy wore all black, a dark suit jacket, the top button of his shirt undone and tie loose. He wore his brown hair almost shoulder length and swept back from his face to reveal a strong, square jaw.

A jaw far more familiar than any shoes. Nerves danced in her stomach far faster than even the partiers gyrating to the live band on the boat.

He pivoted on his heel, facing her full on, the moonlight glinting off the chestnut hints in his wavy hair. Sunglasses shielded his eyes from her. Shades at night? For a low profile or ego?

Regardless, she knew. Her ex-husband wasn't content with just calling and leaving a message. No, not Jonah. The powerful international scion she'd divorced a year ago had returned.

Jonah Landis whipped off his sunglasses, glanced at his watch and grinned. "Sorry I'm late. Have we missed the party?"

To hell with any party. Jonah Landis wanted to find out why Eloisa hadn't told him the entire truth when she'd demanded a divorce a year ago. He also wanted to know why his passionate lover had so dispassionately cut him off.

The stunned look on Eloisa's face as she stopped cold on the dock would have been priceless if he wasn't so damn mad over the secret she'd kept from him, a secret that he'd only just found out was gumming up the works on their divorce decree.

Of course when he'd met her in Madrid a year ago, he'd been distracted by the instantaneous, mind-blowing chemistry between them. And looking at her now, seeing her quiet elegance, he figured he could cut himself some slack on missing details that could have clued him in—like how much she'd fit into her Spanish surroundings.

The woman was a walking distraction.

Wind molded her tan silk dress around her body. The dimly lit night played tricks with his vision until she looked nearly naked, clothed only in shifting shadows.

Had she known that when she chose the dress? Likely not. Eloisa seemed oblivious to her allure, which only served to enhance her appeal.

Her sleek dark hair was slicked back in a severe ponytail that gave her already exotic brown eyes a tug. Without so much as lip gloss, she relegated most models to the shadows.

Once he had her name on the dotted line of divorce papers—official ones this time—he would have nothing to do with her ever again. That had been the plan anyway. He didn't need round two of her hot-cold treatment. So he'd misread the signs, hadn't realized she was drunk during the "I do" part. That didn't mean she had to slap his face and fall off the planet. He was over Eloisa.

Or so he'd thought. Then he'd seen her and felt that impact all over again, that kick-in-the-gut effect he'd thought must have been exaggerated by his memory.

He tamped back the attraction and focused on seeing this through. He needed her signature and for some reason he refused to leave it up to lawyers. Maybe it had something to do with closure.

Eloisa inched her heel from between the planks and set both feet as firmly as her delicate jaw. "What are you doing here?"

"I came to accompany you to your sister's engagement party." He hooked an elbow on the open limo door, the chauffeur waiting up front as he'd been instructed earlier. "Can't have my wife going stag."

"Shhh!" Lurching toward him, she patted the air in front of his face, stopping just shy of touching his mouth. "I am not your wife."

He clasped her hand, thumb rubbing over her bare

ring finger. "Damn, I must have hallucinated that whole wedding ceremony in Madrid."

Eloisa yanked her hand away and rubbed her palm against her leg. "You're arguing semantics."

"If you would prefer to skip the party, we could grab a bite to eat and talk about those semantics." He watched the glide of her hand up and down her thigh, remembering well the creamy, soft texture under his mouth as he'd tasted his way up.

She stared at him silently until he met her eyes again. "You're kidding, right?"

"Climb into the car and see."

She glanced back at the boat, then at him again, her long ponytail fanning to rest along her shoulder. "I'm not so sure that's a good idea."

"Afraid I'll kidnap you?"

"Don't be ridiculous." She laughed nervously as if she'd considered just that.

"Then what's holding you back? Unless you want to continue this conversation right here." He nodded toward the boat full of partyers. "I thought you wanted me to be quiet."

She looked back over her shoulder again, and while it appeared no one noticed them, who knew how long that would hold? Not that he gave a damn what anyone thought, unlike his enigmatic wife. He'd learned a long time ago he had two choices in this world. Let others rule his life or take charge.

The second option won hands down.

He cocked an eyebrow and waited.

"Fine," she bit out between gritted teeth.

She eyed him angrily as she angled past and slid into

the car without even brushing against him. Eloisa settled into the leather seat.

Jonah tucked himself inside next her, closed the door and tapped the glass window between them and the chauffeur, signaling him to drive. Just drive. He would issue a destination later.

"Where are we going?" she asked as the limo eased into motion, the tinted windows closing them in their own private capsule.

"Where do you want to go? I have a penthouse suite farther down on Pensacola Beach."

"Of course you do." Her gaze flicked around the small space, lingering briefly on his computer workstation to her left before moving on to the minibar and the plasma screen TV.

"I see you haven't changed." He'd forgotten how prickly she could be about money. Still, it had been refreshing. He'd had plenty of women chase him because of the Landis portfolio and political influence.

He'd never had a female dump him because of it. Of course back then he hadn't known she had access to money and influence beyond even his family's reach. Mighty damn impressive.

And confusing since she hadn't bothered to share that even after they married.

He put a damper on the surge of anger, a dangerous emotion given the edge of desire searing his insides. To prove to himself he could stay in control, he slid two fingers down the length of a sleekly straight lock of her black hair.

Eloisa jerked her head away. "Stop that." She adjusted the air-conditioning vent nervously until the blast of air ruffled her ponytail. "Enough playing, although you certainly seem to be an expert at recreation. I just want to know why you're here, now."

With all he knew about her, she still understood so little about him. "What's wrong with wanting to see my wife?"

"Ex-wife. We got drunk and ended up married." She shrugged casually, too much so. "It happens to lots of folks, from pop stars to everyday Joes and Josephines. Just check out the marriage logs in Las Vegas. We made a mistake, but we took steps to fix it the morning after."

"Do you consider all of it a mistake? Even the part between 'I do' and waking up with a hangover?" He couldn't resist reminding her.

A whisper of attraction smoked through her dark eyes. "I don't remember."

"You're blushing," he noted with more than a little satisfaction, grateful for the soft glow of a muted overhead light. So he was smug. Sue him. "You remember the good parts all right."

"Sex is irrelevant." She sniffed primly.

"Sex? I was talking about the food." He turned the tables, enjoying the cat-and-mouse game between them. "The *mariscada en salsa verde* was amazing." And just that fast, he could all but taste the shellfish casserole in green sauce, the supper she'd shared with him before they had after-dinner drinks. Got hitched. Got naked.

He could see the same memory reflected in her eyes just before her mouth pursed tight.

"You're a jackass, Jonah."

"But I'm all yours." For now at least.

"Not anymore. Remember the morning-after 'fix'? You're my *ex*-jackass."

If only it were that simple to put this woman in his past. God knows, he'd tried hard enough over the past year to forget about Eloisa Taylor Landis.

Or rather Eloisa *Medina* Landis?

He'd stumbled upon the glitch in a church registry, a "minor" technicality she'd forgotten to mention, but one that had snarled up their paperwork in Spain. The sense of shock and yeah, even some bitter betrayal rocked through him again.

No question, he needed to put this woman in his past, but this time he would be the one to walk away.

"Now there you're wrong, Eloisa. That fix got broken along the way." He picked up a lock of her hair again, keeping his hand off her shoulder.

Lightly he tugged, making his presence felt. A spark of awareness flickered through her eyes, flaming an answering heat inside him. He looked at the simple gold chain around her neck and remembered the jewels he'd once pictured there while she'd slept. Then she woke up and made it clear there would be no summer together. She couldn't get out of his life fast enough.

Her breath hitched. He reminded himself of his reason for coming here, to end things and leave.

Now he wondered if it might be all the more satisfying to have one last time with Eloisa, to ensure she remembered all they could have had if only she'd been as upfront with him as he'd been with her.

He glided his knuckles up her ponytail to her cheek, gently urging her to face him more fully. "The paperwork never made it through. Something to do with you lying about your name."

Her eyes darted away. "I never lied about my name—" She sat up straighter, her gaze slamming back into his. "What do you mean the paperwork didn't go through?"

She seemed to be genuinely surprised, but he'd learned not to trust her. Still he would play this game out in order to achieve his ultimate goal—a final night in her bed before leaving her forever.

"The divorce wasn't finalized. You, my dear, are still Mrs. Jonah Landis."

Two

He had to be joking.

Eloisa dug her fingers into the leather seats, seriously considering making use of that bottle of bourbon in the limo's minibar. Except indulging in a few too many umbrella drinks had landed her in this mess in the first place.

She'd taken pains to cover her tracks. Her mother had warned her how important it was to be careful. Keep a low profile. Stay above reproach. And never, ever invite scrutiny.

Eloisa looked out the window to see where they were headed. They passed nail salons and T-shirt shops along the beachfront, nightlife in full swing on open-decked restaurant bars. The chauffeur truly seemed like he was simply driving around, not headed anywhere specific—such as Jonah's hotel.

She simply couldn't pay the price for being impulsive again. "We signed the divorce paperwork."

His blue eyes narrowed. "Apparently there's some—thing you neglected to tell me, a secret you've kept mighty close to the vest."

Eloisa bit her lip to hold back impulsive words while she gathered her thoughts and reminded herself to be grateful he hadn't stumbled upon her more recent secret. Her empty stomach gripped with nerves. She tried to draw in calming breaths, but had to face a truth learned long ago. Only when working at the library could she relax.

Best she could tell, there weren't any books conveniently tucked away in this superbly stocked luxury ride. Although the backseat area was packed with enough technology to provide a command central for a small army. Apparently Jonah preferred to have the world at his fingertips. Odd, but she didn't have time for distractions right now.

"What secret?" she asked out of a long-honed habit of denial. To date, no one had pressed the point so the strategy hadn't let her down yet. "I have no idea what you're talking about."

His jaw went tight with irritation. "That's the way you want to play this? Fine." He leaned in closer until she couldn't miss the musky scent of him mixed with his still-familiar aftershave. "You forgot to mention your father."

Her chest went tighter than her hands twisting in the skirt of her dress. "My dad's a tax collector in Pensacola, Florida. Speaking of which, why aren't you home in Hilton Head, South Carolina?"

He gripped her wrists to stop her nervous fidgeting. "Not your stepdad, your biological father."

Apparently, Jonah wasn't easily diverted tonight.

"I told you before about my biological father." A shiver passed over her at even the mention of the man who'd wrecked her mother's life, the man she lied about on a regular basis. "My mother was a single parent when I was born. My real father was a bum who wanted no part in my life." True enough.

Her dad—no more than a sperm donor as far as she was concerned—had broken her mother's heart then left her to raise their child alone. Her stepfather might not have been Prince Charming—wasn't that damn ironic?—but at least he'd been there for her and her mother.

"A bum? A royal bum." Jonah stretched a leg out in front of him, polished snakeskin loafer gleaming in the overhead lamp. "Interesting dichotomy."

She squeezed her eyes shut and wished it was that easy to shut out the repercussions of what he'd somehow discovered. Her mother had been emphatic about personal safety. Her biological father still had enemies back in San Rinaldo. She'd been foolish to tempt fate by going to Spain in hopes of unobtrusively learning about half her heritage on the small island country nearby. Damn it all, fear was a good thing when it kept a person safe.

She steadied her breath, if not her galloping heart rate. "Would you please not say that?"

"Say what?"

"The whole *royal* thing." While her stepfather frequently called Audrey his "little princess," he—and the rest of the world—didn't know that Eloisa was actually the one with royal blood singing through her veins, thanks to her biological father.

Nobody knew, except Eloisa, her deceased mother and a lawyer who conducted any communication with the deposed king. Eloisa's so-called real father. A man still hunted to this day by the rebel faction that had taken over his small island kingdom of San Rinaldo off the coast of Spain.

How had Jonah found out?

He tipped her chin with one knuckle as his driver slowed for jaywalking teens. "You may have been able to fool the world for a lot of years, but I've figured out your secret. You're the illegitimate daughter of deposed King Enrique Medina."

She stiffened defensively, then forced herself to relax nonchalantly. "That's ridiculous." Albeit true. If he could figure it out, how much longer until her secret was revealed to others? She needed to know, hopefully find some way to plug that leak and persuade him he was wrong.

Then she would decide what to do if his claim was actually true, a notion that could have her hyperventilating if she thought about it too long. "What makes you think something so outlandish?"

"I discovered the truth when I went back to Europe recently. My brother and his wife decided to renew their wedding vows and while I was in the area, I stopped by the chapel where we got married."

A bolt of surprise shot through her and she couldn't help but think back to that night. She'd been emotionally flattened by her mother's death and had only just returned to finish her studies in Europe. She'd shared some drinks with the guy she'd secretly had a crush on and the next thing she'd known, they were hunting for a preacher or a justice of the peace with the lights still on.

Visiting the place where they'd exchanged vows sounded sentimental. Like that day meant more to him than a drunken mistake.

She couldn't stop herself from asking, "You went back there?"

"I was in the neighborhood," he repeated, his jaw going tight, the first sign that the whole debacle may have upset him as much as it had her.

He'd let her go so easily, agreeing they'd made an impulsive mistake rather than asking her to crawl back in bed with him and discuss it later. A huge part of her had wanted him to sweep away rational concerns. But no. He'd let her leave, just as her father never claimed her mother.

Or her.

She tore her eyes away from the tempting curve of his mouth, a mouth that had brought such intense pleasure when he'd explored every patch of her skin later that night after their "I do." Except they'd exchanged vows in Spanish, which had seemed romantic at the time. Between her hiccups. "Everyone knows King Enrique doesn't live in San Rinaldo anymore. Nobody knows where he and his sons fled after they left. There are only rumors."

"Rumors that he's in Argentina." Jonah lounged back in the seat, seemingly lazy and relaxed, except for the coiled muscles she could see bunched under his black jacket.

She knew well he came by those muscles honestly. Her first memory of him was burned in her brain, the day she'd joined the restoration team on a graduate internship to assist with research. Jonah had been studying blueprints with another man on the construction site. She'd mistakenly thought Jonah worked on the crew, from his casual clothes and mud-stained boots. The guy was actually a couple of credits away from his PhD. He wasn't just an architect, he was a bit of an artist in his own right.

That had enticed her.

Only later, too late for her own good, had she discovered who he was. A Landis, a member of a financial and political dynasty.

Eloisa looked away from his too-perceptive eyes and swept her hem back over her knees. "I wouldn't know anything about that."

Lying came so easily after this long.

"It also appears that neither you nor your mother has been to Argentina, but that's not my point." His eyes drilled into her until she looked back at him. "I don't give a damn where your royal papa lives. I'm only concerned with the fact that you lied to me, which gummed up the works for our divorce."

"Okay, then." She met his gaze defiantly. "If what you say is true, maybe it means the marriage is void, too, so we don't need a divorce."

He shook his head. "No such luck. I checked. Believe me. We are totally and completely husband and wife."

Jonah slid his fingers down the length of her hair until his hand cupped her hip. His hand rested warm and familiar and tempting against her until she could swear she felt his calluses through her dress. She struggled not to squirm—or sway closer.

She clasped his wrist and set his hand back on his

knee. "File abandonment charges. Or I will. I don't care as long as this is taken care of quickly and quietly. No one here knows about my, uh, impetuosity."

"Don't you want to discuss who gets the china and who gets the monogrammed towels?"

Argh! She tapped on the window. "Driver? Driver?" She kept rapping until the window parted. "Take me back now, please."

The chauffeur glanced at Jonah who nodded curtly.

His autocratic demeanor made her want to scream out her frustration but she wouldn't cause a scene. Why did this man alone have the power to make her blood boil? She was a master of calm. Everyone said so, from the stodgiest of library board members to her sixth grade track coach who never had managed to coax her to full speed.

She waited until the window closed before turning to him again. "You can have every last bit of the nothing I own if you'll please just stop this madness now. Arguing isn't going to solve anything. I'll have my lawyer look into the divorce issue."

That was as close as she would come to admitting he'd stumbled on the truth. She certainly couldn't outright confirm it without seeing what proof he had and hopefully have time to take it to her attorney. Too many lives were at stake. There were still people out there tied to the group that tried to assassinate Enrique Medina, had in fact succeeded in killing his wife, the mother of his three legitimate heirs.

Enrique had been a widower when he met her mother in Florida, and still they hadn't gotten married. Her mom vowed she hadn't wanted any part of the royal lifestyle, but her jaw had always quivered when she said it. Right now Eloisa sympathized with her mother more than she could have ever imagined. Relationships were damn complicated—and painful.

Thank goodness the limo approached the paddleboat again because she didn't know how much more of this she could take tonight. The car stopped smoothly alongside the dock.

"Jonah, if that's all you have to say, I need to return to the party. My attorney will be in touch with you first thing next week."

Eloisa reached for the door.

His hand fell to rest on top of hers, his body pressing intimately against her as he stretched past.

"Hold on a minute. Do you really think I'm letting you out of my sight again that easily? Last time I did that, you ditched before lunch. I'm not wasting another year looking for you if you decide to bolt."

"I didn't run. I came home to Pensacola." She tried to inch free but he clasped her hands in his. "This is where you can find me."

Where he could have found her anytime over the past twelve months if he'd cared at all. In the first few weeks she'd waited, hoped, then the panic set in as she'd wrestled with contacting him.

Now, they had no reason to talk.

"I'm here now." His thumb stroked the inside of her wrist. "And we're going to fix this mess face-to-face rather than trusting the system again."

"No!" Already her skin tingled with awareness so much more intense than when he'd cupped her hip—and she'd been mighty aware.

Damn her traitorous body.

"Yes," he said, reaching past and throwing open the door.

He was letting her go after all? But hadn't he just said they were going to confront things face-to-face?

However, who was she to waste time questioning the reason he'd changed his mind? She rushed out of the limousine and turned at the last second to say goodbye to Jonah. Why was her gut clenching at the notion of never seeing him again?

She pivoted on her heel only to slam into his chest. Apparently he'd stepped out of the vehicle as well. Distant voices from her sister's party drifted on the wind, something she could barely register since his sun-bronzed face lowered toward hers.

Before she could breathe, much less protest, his mouth covered hers. His eyes stayed open, which she realized must mean hers were open, too. Just like a year ago, she stared at his eyes, the kind of blue poets wrote about. His wild and fresh nature scent was the same sort evoked by a literary walk through Thoreau's *Walden*.

And just that fast, her lashes fluttered closed. She savored the taste of him on her lips, her tongue again. Her hands slid up to splay on his chest, hard muscles rippling under her fingers.

Then unease niggled at the back of her brain, a sense of unrest. Something was off about this kiss. She remembered what it was like to be kissed by Jonah, and as nerve tingling as it felt to be pressed against him, to inhale the scent of him, this wasn't right.

She tried to gather her thoughts enough to think rationally rather than just languish in sensation. His broad hand moved along her waist, lightly, rhythmically.

Totally in control.

Where everyone could see.

He was putting on a display for the partyers on the boat, damn him. Indignation, anger and a hint of hurt smoked through her veins, chasing away desire. She started to pull back then reconsidered. The damage was already done. Everyone at the party had seen them kiss. They would assume the worst. She might as well take advantage of the opportunity to surprise Jonah for a change. And yes, even to extract a little revenge for how he'd staged this whole encounter tonight to knock her off balance rather than simply notifying her through their attorneys.

Eloisa slid her arms around his waist, not that anyone could see behind him. But what she was about to do wasn't for public viewing anyway.

It was all for Jonah.

Eloisa grabbed his butt.

Jonah blinked in surprise, her hand damn near searing through his pants. He started to pull away…then sensation steamrolled over him. This kiss wasn't going the way he'd planned. He certainly hadn't expected her to take control of the game he'd started.

Now that she had? Time to turn the tables again.

Gasps of surprise drifting on the wind from the boat, he cupped her neck and stroked his tongue along the seam of her lips, just once, but enough, if the hitch in her breathing was anything to judge by. Her body turned fluid as she pressed closer to him. Her hands skimmed up along his spine to his shoulders. Then she speared her fingers through his hair, sending his pulse spiking and placing his self-control on shaky ground.

Without question, he wanted to take this encounter

further, but not here. Not in public. And he knew if they moved to the limo, reason would pull her away again. So with more than a little regret, he ended the kiss. He'd made his point anyway.

Jonah eased away from her, still keeping his hands looped behind her back in case she decided to bolt—or slap him. "We'll finish this later, princess, when we don't have an audience."

When he could take this to the natural finish his body demanded. And when she was totally consenting rather than merely acting on impulse. The kiss may have started as a staged way to make her family aware of their connection, but halfway in, he'd realized his instincts were dead-on.

He couldn't walk away without one last time in her bed.

Her lips pursed tight as if holding back a retort, but her hands shook as she slid them from behind him to rest on his chest. He watched over her shoulder as a small group left the boat and started toward them on the boardwalk. A trio led the pack. Thanks to photos from an investigator, Jonah IDed the three right away. Her stepfather, Harry Taylor. Her half sister, Audrey Taylor. And Audrey's fiancé, Joey.

Eloisa leaned closer and whispered through tight teeth. "You are so going to pay for doing this."

"Shhh." He dropped a quick kiss on her forehead, liking the taste of his revenge so far. His appetite for it—for her—only increased the longer he spent by her side. "We don't want them to hear us fighting, do we, dear?"

Jonah slipped his arm around her shoulders and

tucked her by his side, her soft curves pressed enticingly against him.

She stiffened. "You can't be planning to tell them... uh..."

"About your father?"

Her brown eyes flashed with warring anger and fear. "About your theories. About you and me."

"My lips are sealed, princess."

"Stop calling me that," she said through gritted teeth as the footsteps thunked louder and closer.

"You and I both know it's true. There's no more denying it. The only question is, how far will you go to keep me quiet?"

She gasped. "You can't mean—"

"Too late to talk, Eloisa dear." He squeezed her lightly as the group closed in, her family leading. "Trust me or not."

The older man in the lead fanned a hand over his wind-blown blond hair, whisper thin along the top. His daughter—the bride to be—was an even paler version of her father. Even her hair seemed bleached white by the sun, yet she didn't sport even a hint of a tan. Her fiancé hovered behind, fists shoved in his pockets. He shuffled from foot to foot as if impatient to be anywhere but here. A small crowd gathered behind them while others watched from the deck railing.

Jonah extended his hand to Eloisa's stepfather. "Sorry I'm late, sir. I'm Eloisa's date for tonight's shindig. I'm Jonah Landis."

She wouldn't be able to dismiss him as easily this time.

Harry Taylor's eyes widened. "Landis? As in the Landises from Hilton Head, South Carolina?"

"Yes, sir, that would be my family."

"Uh, Harry Taylor, here. Eloisa's father."

The guy all but had dollar signs flashing in his pupils like some cartoon character.

Jonah stifled the irritation for Eloisa's sake. He appreciated the advantages his family's money had brought him, but he preferred to make his own way in the world.

Meanwhile, though, Jonah knew how to deal with money suck-ups like this. He'd been on guard against them since the sandbox. Even kids figured out fast whose dad had the biggest portfolio.

A photographer stepped from the back of the pack, lifting the lens to his eyes. Eloisa tucked behind his shoulder as flashes spiked through the night.

Smiling widely, Harry shuffled aside to clear the way for the photographer to get a better angle. The old guy all but offered to hold the photographer's camera bag.

Audrey elbowed her yawning fiancé, hooking arms with him and stepping closer. "When did you and Eloisa meet, Mr. Landis? I'm sure our guest—the editor of the local events section of our illustrious paper—will want plenty of deets for her column."

"Call me Jonah." He could feel Eloisa's heart beat faster against him.

He could claim her easily here, but then their separation would be out in the open as well. He intended to be much closer to her. "I met Eloisa during her study-abroad program last year. I found her impossible to forget and here I am."

Every word of that was true.

Eloisa's sigh of relief shuddered against him.

Audrey loosened her death grip on her fiancé's arm

long enough to sidle beside her sister for the next round of pictures. "Aren't you full of surprises?"

"Not by choice." Eloisa smiled tightly. "Besides, this is your night. I wouldn't want to do anything to detract from that."

Her stepsister winked, eying Jonah up and down. "Hey, if he were my date, I'd be lapping up all the media attention."

What the hell kind of family was this?

Jonah pulled Eloisa closer to his side, sending a clear "back-off" signal to Audrey. She simply smiled in return, tossing her hair over her shoulders playfully. Her fiancé seemed oblivious, poor bastard.

Eloisa buried her face against Jonah's shoulder and he started to reassure her—until he realized she wasn't upset or even seeking him out. She was just hiding from the clicking camera.

The photographer snap, snap, snapped away, the flashes damn near blinding in the dark night.

Audrey reached for her sister. "Come on. Just smile for the camera. You've been hiding out here all night and I could use some fun and interesting pictures to add to my wedding album."

Eloisa thumbed off the band from her ponytail. Her hair slid free in a silken sheet that flowed over her shoulders and down her back. She'd never seemed vain to him, but then most women he knew primped for the camera. Even his three sisters-in-law were known to slick on lipstick before a news conference.

Except as he watched her more closely he realized she used the hair as a curtain. The guy might be getting his photos—to deny them would have caused a scene with

Audrey—but there wasn't going to be a clear image of Eloisa's face.

Realization trickled through of a larger problem between them than even he had anticipated. He knew she wanted to keep her royal heritage a secret. That was obvious enough and he respected her right to live as she pleased. But until this moment he hadn't understood just how far she would go to protect her anonymity. A damned inconvenient problem.

Because as a Landis, he could always count on being stuck in the spotlight. Just by being with her, he'd cast her into the media's unrelenting glare.

He'd wanted revenge, but didn't need to unveil her secret to repay her for her betrayal. He had other, far more enticing ways of excising her from his mind.

Three

Eloisa wished that photographer would tone down the flash on his camera. Much more of his nonstop shutter bugging and she would have a headache. As if this evening wasn't already migraine material enough.

Thank God the party had finally all but ended, only a few stragglers hanging on and sidling into the photo ops. Jonah—the cause of her impending headache—stood off to the side with her stepfather. Determined to keep her cool, Eloisa stacked tiny crystal cake plates left haphazardly on the dessert table. Her sister watched from her perch, lounging against the end of the table.

Audrey balanced a plate with a wedge of the raspberry chocolate cake on one hand, swiping her finger through the frosting and licking it clean. "You should let the catering staff take care of that. It's what they're paid to do."

"I don't mind, really. Besides, the cleaning staff charges by the hour." She also needed a way to burn off her nervous energy from Jonah's staged kiss.

"That doesn't mean you need to work yourself to the bone. Go home."

She wasn't ready to be alone with Jonah. Not yet. Not with her feelings still so close to the surface. But judging from the stubborn set of his jaw as he stood under a string of white lights, he wasn't leaving her life anywhere anytime soon.

"I'm staying here with you." Eloisa sidestepped a band member carrying two guitar cases. "No arguments."

"At least have some cake. It's so amazing I almost don't care that I'll have to get my wedding gown resized." Audrey swiped up another gob of frosting, her blue eyes trekking over to Jonah, then sliding back. "You're just full of surprises, aren't you, sister dear?"

"So you said earlier." Eloisa placed the forks in a glass so all the plates stacked evenly and handed over the lot to a passing catering employee.

How rare that someone accused her of being full of surprises. She'd always been the steady one, tasked to smooth things over when her more-sensitive baby sister burst into tears.

"But it's true. What's the scoop with this Landis boyfriend?" Audrey gestured with her plate toward Jonah who looked at ease in his suit jacket, even in Florida's full-out May heat.

Eloisa had found his constant unconcern fascinating before. Now it was more than a little irritating, especially when she couldn't stop thinking about the feel of plunging her fingers into his thick hair when they'd kissed.

She forced her hands to stay steady as she clasped them in front of her, leaning against the table beside Audrey, her half sister topping her by five inches. Her willowy sister looked more like her blond father.

But they both had their mother's long fingers. What would it have been like to turn to her mother right now? And how much it must hurt Audrey not having their mother around to help plan the biggest day of her life.

Certainly their mother's shocking death from an allergic reaction to medication had stunned them all. Eloisa had been numb throughout the entire funeral, staying in the fugue state all the way back to Spain, to her study program.

And into Jonah's bed.

Waking up the morning after with that ring on her finger... She'd felt the first crack in the dam walling up her grief. She'd barely made it out of Jonah's rented manor home before the tears flowed.

Which brought her back to the dilemma of Jonah.

What was the scoop? Why had he shown up now when he could have sent a lawyer? It wasn't like he wanted to see her or he could have contacted her anytime in the past year. "His arrival tonight came as a total shocker to me."

Audrey set aside her plate, plucked a pink stargazer lily from the beach-themed centerpiece and skimmed it under her nose. "You never mentioned meeting him before."

She hadn't mentioned even the working relationship because she'd been afraid they would hear in her voice what she could barely admit to herself then, much less now. "Like I said earlier, this is your time, your wedding. I wouldn't want to do anything to distract from that."

Audrey bumped her waif-thin shoulder against Eloisa's. "Could you please drop the altruistic gig for just a few minutes while we squeal over this like real sisters? He's a Landis, for crying out loud. You're rubbing elbows with American royalty."

"Who wouldn't squeal over that?" She couldn't resist the tongue-in-cheek retort.

"You, apparently." Audrey twirled the lily stem between her fingers. "Heaven knows I would be calling a press conference."

Eloisa laughed, then laughed some more, so much better than crying, and let all the tension from the evening flow out of her. Audrey had her faults, but she never pretended to be anything other than who she was.

Which made Eloisa feel like a hypocrite since she hid from herself every damn day.

Her laughter faded. "Forget all about this evening and Jonah Landis. I meant it when I said these next couple of weeks are totally about you. This is the wedding you've been planning since you were a kid. Remember how we used to practice in the garden?"

"You were always the best maid of honor." She tucked the stargazer lily behind Eloisa's ear. "I wasn't always a nice bride."

"You were three years younger. You got frustrated when you couldn't keep up."

"I still do sometimes." Her smile faltered just a bit.

"Remember the time we picked all the roses off the bushes?" Eloisa steadied the lily behind her ear, the fragrance reminding her of their childhood raid on their mother's carefully tended yard. "You took the rap."

Audrey rolled her eyes and attacked her cake again

with her pointer finger. "No huge sacrifice. It's not like I ever got in trouble. I cried better than you did. You were always into being stoic."

"I'm not the weepy sort." Not in public anyway.

"Tears can be worth their weight in gold. I may be the youngest, but you should take my advice on this one." Audrey fixed her stare on her father, her fiancé and Jonah. "When it comes to men, you have to use whatever tools you have."

"Thanks for the advice." Not that she could see herself taking it even in a million years. "Now can we get back to focusing on your wedding? We have a lot to accomplish in the next couple of weeks."

She tried to stem her reservations about Audrey marrying a guy with questionable connections. Her little sister had ignored all the warnings, even threatening to elope if Eloisa didn't keep her opinions to herself.

Audrey pulled another flower from the centerpiece for herself. "And about Jonah Landis?"

Eloisa shrugged, suddenly hungry for the cake after all. "He's my date." She forked up a bite from the lone remaining slice on a plate the caterers hadn't yet cleared. "It's as simple as that."

"Guess you don't need a ride home tonight." Audrey needled with the same practiced teasing she'd used on her since the days of Eloisa's first boyfriend—the librarian's son who occasionally snitched the keys to the reference room so she could read the Oxford English Dictionary in total privacy after hours.

"I have my car here."

"One of Joey's brothers can drive it over for you." Audrey arched up on her toes. "Hey, Landis? My sister is ready to go. How about you get your chauffeur to pull up that Rolls Royce limo of yours. Eloisa's been on her feet all day."

Jonah's gaze slammed into hers, narrow and predatory. She'd seen that look before, right before she'd shimmied out of her dress and fallen into bed with him.

Shoveling a bite of cake into her mouth, Eloisa tried to tell herself it would be enough to stave off the deeper hunger gnawing through her tonight.

Eloisa shifted uneasily in the limo seat.

Climbing back into Jonah's car had seemed easier than discussing driving arrangements in front of the gossip rag reporter. Now that she was alone with Jonah, however, she questioned her decision. The drive to her town house felt hours away rather than a couple of miles.

Searching for something, *anything* to talk about other than each other, Eloisa touched the miniprinter and laptop computer beside her. She started to make a joke about checking Facebook from the road, but paused when her finger snagged on a printed-out page.

She looked closer before she could think to stop herself. It seemed like some kind of small blueprint—

Jonah pulled the paper from the printer and into a briefcase. "Why were you so camera shy at the party earlier?"

"I prefer to keep a low profile. Not everyone is hungry for a spot on the front page." Ouch. That sounded pretty crabby coming out, but Jonah had a way of agitating her every nerve.

"Do you avoid the press because of your father? You can't expect to stay under the radar forever."

Did he realize how intimately their thighs pressed

against one another? Eloisa slid her hand from the printer and scooted an inch of space between them. "My mother and I managed over the years. Do you intend to change that?"

She bit her lip, unable to stop from holding her breath after finally voicing the question that had chewed at her all night long. Her mother may have managed but it didn't escape Eloisa's notice that she'd screwed up mere days after the funeral. She waited through Jonah's assessing silence so long that dots began to spark in front of her eyes.

"Breathe," he commanded, holding her gaze until she exhaled then nodding curtly. "Of course I'll keep your secret. If anyone finds out, it won't be from me."

Sighing with relief she flopped back in her seat and fanned her face, relaxing for the first time since she'd heard his engine growl around the corner. That was one secret taken care of, and she had no reason to believe he could have found out her other. "You really could have saved me a lot of angst tonight if you'd told me that from the start."

"What kind of guy do you think I am?"

A rich one judging by his clothes, his lifestyle and famous surname? Yet all of those were superficial elements. She scoured her mind for things she'd learned about him a year ago…and most of it focused on attraction. She wasn't so sure she liked what that said about her. "I'm not really sure how well I know you."

"Then you'll have the next two weeks to figure me out."

"Two weeks?" Her muscles kinked all over again. "I thought you wanted a divorce."

"I do." He secured the lily behind her ear, his knuckles

caressing her neck for a second too long to be accidental. "But first, I want the honeymoon we never had."

She gasped in surprise, followed by anger…then suspicion. "You're just trying to shock me."

"How do you know I'm not serious?" His blue eyes burned with unmistakable, unsettling—irresistible?— desire.

She'd barely survived their last encounter with her heart intact. No way in hell was she dipping her toes into those fiery waters again. "You can't really believe I'll just crawl into bed with you."

"Why not?" He angled closer to her, so close she would only have to lean just a little to rest her cheek against his amazing hair. "It isn't like we haven't already slept together."

Not that they'd slept much. "That night was a mistake." One with heartbreaking consequences. "A mistake I do not intend to repeat, so get back on your side of the car."

"Fine then." He eased away, leather creaking at his every lazy, slow movement. "Whether or not we have sex will be your call."

"Thank you." She laced her fingers together on her lap to keep from hauling him over again. Why hadn't she eaten more cake?

"Just give me two weeks."

"What the hell?" The words slipped out of her mouth, startling her as much as it appeared she'd surprised him. "I can't deal with you right now." There. She'd actually been honest with him about how she felt. "My sister needs me."

And then she had to muck it up with a half truth to hide how much he tempted her.

"Doesn't she have a wedding planner or something?"

"Not everyone has unlimited funds."

"Your father doesn't send support?"

"That's none of your business, and regardless, it wouldn't have been Audrey's anyhow."

"Ah, but if you had a king's ransom tucked away, I am certain you would have shared it with sister dear. Am I wrong?"

His words stung and she hated how that hinted at his power over her. "I'm not a pushover."

Although Jonah was right, damn him, that if she did have money, she would have written her sister a big fat check to cover wedding expenses.

Regardless, she didn't want Enrique Medina's money. Her mother had insisted she didn't want it either, but she'd married another man for what appeared to be financial security. What a confusing tangle.

She knew one thing for sure. "I'm not a minor. I make my own way in the world. Besides, he's not a part of my life and I am not for sale."

She wouldn't allow herself to be dependent on any man. Even months after the fact, it scared her to her teeth to think of how close she'd come to mirroring her mother's past—alone, unloved.

And pregnant.

Four

Jonah told the driver to wait, then pivoted toward Eloisa as she raced toward her town house. Hopefully he would be sending the driver on his way soon, because quite frankly, he didn't trust Eloisa not to bolt the second he left.

Not that it was any great hardship to be with her. God, he could watch her walk all night long, the gentle sway of her hips and the swish of her ponytail illuminated by the street lamp.

He didn't expect to get any further than talking tonight. He needed to take his time with her now in a way he hadn't back in Spain.

Problem was? He could only afford to take these next two weeks off, then he needed to get back to work on his next restoration project. Working on architectural designs around the world fed his wanderer's spirit.

Next stop? Peru in two weeks.

And if he hadn't finished business with Eloisa by then? Could he just walk away?

He refused to consider failure. They would go to bed together again. And they would exorcise the mess from last year.

Hands stuffed in his pockets, he followed Eloisa along the walkway. Waves rolled and roared in the distance, the shore three streets away. She lived in a stucco town house, the fourth in the row. New, they'd been built to resemble older, turn-of-the-century construction. Each unit was painted a different beachy color—peach, blue, green and yellow.

She marched toward the yellow home, calling back over her shoulder. "Thank you for seeing me safely to my front stoop, but you're free to leave now."

"Not so fast, my dear wife." He stopped alongside Eloisa at her lime-green door. Keys dangled from between her fingers but he didn't take them from her. He wanted her to ask him inside of her own free will, no coercion. But that didn't exclude persuasion.

She faced him with a sigh. "You managed a whole year without speaking to me. I'm sure you'll do just fine without me for another night."

"Eloisa, just because I didn't contact you doesn't mean I stopped thinking about you." That was sure as hell the truth. "We left a lot unsaid. Is it so wrong for me to want these next couple of weeks to clear the air before we say goodbye?"

Eloisa studied her clunky key chain, a conglomeration of whistles, a lanyard from some children's festival and a metal touristy-looking token. "Why a couple of weeks?"

Damn. It wouldn't be that persuasive to say that was all the time he had available to pencil her into his work schedule. His brother Sebastian's marriage had fallen apart because of his insane hours at his law practice.

"That's how long my attorney says it will take to get the ball rolling." He'd asked for Sebastian's help this time, as he should have done a year ago. "You can't blame me for wondering if you will disappear again."

Sure the morning after their spur of the moment wedding, they'd both agreed it was a mistake. Okay, they'd both agreed after she'd slapped him. Then she'd gasped in horror and yanked on her clothes as she'd stumbled toward the door. He'd expected once she cooled down, they would at least talk about things, maybe take a step back—a few steps back.

Except once she'd left his place in Spain, she'd ignored any further communication other than mailing the paperwork his way. So actually, the crummy paperwork was her fault.

And his. He couldn't deny it. He shouldn't have been so damn proud he didn't show his lawyer brother Sebastian.

Jonah tugged the dangling keys from her loose grip, sifting the bulk in his hands. The touristy token caught his attention. He looked closer and found…an ironwork reproduction of the house he'd worked on restoring the previous summer. Interesting. Encouraging. "Nice key chain."

"I keep it as a reminder of the risks of impulsiveness." She tugged her keys back, gripping them so tightly her fingers turned bloodlessly white.

"Risks?" Anger kicked around in his gut. She was the one who'd walked out, after all. Not him. "Seems like you walked away mighty damn easily. If it wasn't for this inconvenient legal snafu—" not to mention her lies "—you would have gotten away scot-free."

"Scot-free?" Her face went pale in the moonlight. "You can't possibly think this didn't affect me. You have no idea how deeply I've wrestled with what we did, the mistake we made."

Confusion dulled the edge of his anger. She'd left. She'd never called. Why the hell had she been hiding out if their time together stayed with her this heavily?

"Well, Eloisa? What do you say we make every effort possible to put this to rest once and for all? For the next couple of weeks, you can just call me roomie."

She gasped. "You can't really expect to bunk at my place?"

"Of course not." Jonah focused on the little piece of memorabilia on her key chain, a sign that she'd remembered and even cared. He let her relax for a second before retorting, "I could phone the chauffeur and we could be taken to my beachside suite."

Shaking her head, she slid the key into the lock. "You're outrageous."

He clapped a hand over his chest with a half smile. "That hurt. I prefer to think I'm being considerate to my wife's needs."

"I'm just dying to hear how you reached that conclusion." Shaking her head, she pushed her front door open and stepped inside without giving him the boot.

He took that as an invitation and followed. Victory pulsing inside him, he checked out the space she called home for clues about her. The more he knew the better his chances. He wouldn't make the same mistake again of letting her keep him in the dark.

The living area was airy and open with high ceilings in keeping with the historic-reproduction feel. Her tastes ran to uncluttered, clean lines with a beach theme— white walls, wood floors and rattan furniture with cushions in a muted blue, tan and chocolate. And of course books—in end tables, shelves, curio cabinets. She'd always carried books in her purse in Spain, reading during breaks.

Her reed roll-up shades covered the windows from outdoor eyes. Only the French doors gave a glimpse to a garden patio with an Adirondack chair and ferns. Did she lounge there and read? Soak up the sun?

What he wouldn't give to take her to his penthouse suite with a rooftop pool and deck where they both could do away with restrictive bathing suits.

He slid his jacket off and hooked it on the coatrack made from a canoe paddle. "Nice place."

"I'm sure it's not near the luxury level you're used to, but I like it."

"It's lovely and you know it. Don't paint me as a bad guy here just to make it easier to dismiss me."

She glanced back over her shoulder, her purse sliding from her shoulder onto the island counter separating the kitchen from the living space. She tossed her keys beside the bag, the cluster jangling to rest. "Fair enough."

He'd spent more than a few nights in tents or trailers during the early, intense stages of a restoration project, but he didn't intend to make excuses to her. "Would you like more luxury in your life?"

His brothers showered their wives with pampering extras and while his sisters-in-law vowed they didn't need them, he'd noticed they always used those spa gifts.

He thumbed a thick silver binder with an engagement photo of Audrey Taylor and her fiancé. "You said earlier you're swamped with wedding plans." He tapped the three-ring binder. "If we stay at my suite, you won't have to cook or clean. You can indulge in the spa. A massage would take care of your stress at the end of the day. You and your sister and all the bridesmaids could avail yourselves of the salon the day of the wedding, my gift to the bride, of course."

She slid out of her gold strappy heels and lined them up side by side on the floor mat by the patio door. "You can't buy me off any more than my father could."

He took his cue from her and toed off his python loafers, nudging them near the coatrack. How much further could they take this undressing together? "I was brought up to believe it's not what a gift costs, it's whether or not the gift is thoughtful. Needed."

"That's nice." She relaxed a hip against a barstool.

"Then pack your bag and let's go to my penthouse."

She stiffened again. "I'm not leaving."

"Then I guess I'm bunking on your sofa." He stifled a wince at spending the night on the couch at least six inches too short.

"You can't tell me you actually wanted me to stay together?" Her eyes went wider with shock. "Every woman on that site in Madrid knew what a playboy you are."

"Were. I'm a married man now." He still had his ring and hers in a jeweler's box in his suite. He wasn't sure why he'd brought them.

She shook her head slowly with a weary sigh. "I'm too tired for this tonight, Jonah. Go back to your hotel. We'll talk tomorrow when we've both had a good night's sleep."

"Honestly? I don't trust you."

"Excuse me?" she gasped in outrage.

Then something else shadowed through her eyes. Guilt?

"You didn't tell me about your father, a pretty major part of your past. You may have done a damn fine job hiding the truth over the years. But when my divorce attorney compared the information you filed on our marriage license at the church registry with your passport information, he found a red flag in the slightly different way you listed your name and your parents. He dug deeper and found your birth certificate. The original one, not the one reissued when Harry Taylor adopted you." The shock he'd felt upon discovering the whole mess roared back to life inside him. "With a little help from a private detective, the rest of the pieces fell into place about your real father. I'm surprised you got away with it for this long."

"You had no right to send private detectives snooping into my private business."

Her words stoked his barely banked anger. "I'm your husband. I think that gives me a little latitude here. For God's sake, Eloisa, what if I'd gotten married again, thinking we were divorced?"

"Are you seeing someone else?" Wow, she sure had

that prim librarian gig down pat. She could have stared down an armed gang.

"Hell no, I'm not seeing anyone else." He couldn't keep himself from comparing other women to her and they all came up short. "Bottom line? Like I said, I don't trust you. You ran once before. I intend to stick close until we have this settled."

She pointed to the binder. "I have my sister's wedding. I'm not going anywhere."

"There are a lot of ways to lock a person out of your life." He'd seen his brother Sebastian and his wife put a massive chasm between each other while living in the same town.

"You can't really expect to stay here, in my town house."

He would have preferred they stay in his suite where he could have wooed her with all the resort offered, but sleeping under the same roof would suffice.

Jonah picked up her keys from the island and held them up so the Spanish charm caught the light. "We both have a lot of unresolved business to settle in two weeks. We should make the most of every minute."

She stared at the keys in his hand for so long he wondered if she was halfway hypnotized.

Finally, Eloisa pressed her fingers to her forehead. "Fine. I'm too tired to argue with you. You can stay, but—" she held up a finger, the stern glint in her eyes relaying loud and clear she was done compromising for the night "—you'll be sleeping on the sofa."

All the same he couldn't resist teasing her, suddenly needing to see if her smile was as blinding as he remembered. "No welcome-home nookie?"

She frowned. "Don't push your luck."

"A guy can still hope." He turned on a lamp, his gaze dropping to the glass paperweight sealing off a dried rose and seashell. He scooped it up, tossed it, caught it, tossed, caught...

"Could you put that down, please?" she snapped with an edge to her voice he hadn't heard since the morning she'd left.

He looked back at the paperweight in his hand. Was it something sentimental? A gift from another guy perhaps? He didn't like the swift kick of jealousy, but damn it all, she was his wife, for now at least. "Should I be worried about a boyfriend showing up to kick my ass?"

"Let's talk about you instead. What have you been up to over the past year, thinking you were a bachelor?"

"Jealous?" God knows he was because she hadn't answered his question. Except if there had been another guy, surely he would have been at the party with her tonight.

His conclusion wasn't proof positive, but he took comfort in it all the same.

She snatched the paperweight from his hand. "I am tired, *not* jealous."

Did he want her to be? No. He wanted honesty. So he settled for the same from himself. "I've spent the past twelve months pining for my ex-wife."

As much as he'd meant to be a sarcastic joke, it hadn't come out of his mouth the way he'd planned.

Confusion flickered through her dark eyes. "The way you say that, I can almost believe you. Of course I know better."

"I thought you said we barely knew each other. We only spent a month together. And we spent most of the time in bed." He sat on the sofa, stretching his arm along the back. "Let's talk now."

"You first." She perched on the edge of the chair beside the sofa.

"You already know plenty about me. My family's in the news and what you don't see there you can find on Wikipedia." He watched her chest rise and fall faster with nerves, lending further credence to his sense she disliked anything high profile.

"None of that information tells me anything reliable about who you are." She counted on her fingers. "I remember you were always on time for work. You never talked on your cell phone when you spoke with the foreman on the site. I liked that you gave people your full attention. I remember you downplayed the Landis connection so well I didn't even know you were related until three weeks into the job." She folded her fingers down again. "But Jonah, that's not enough reason to get married. Even with the divorce, we have a history now. We should know more about each other than our work habits."

"I know you like two sugars in your coffee," he offered with a half smile.

This didn't seem the right time to mention he knew her heart beat faster when he blew along the inside curve of her neck. The sex part would have to wait.

Talking appeared to be the only way to get closer to her, so he would talk. "You want to know more about me? Okay. My brother Kyle got married recently."

"You mentioned that already when you talked about their vows renewal."

"They went to Portugal, which is how I ended up in Spain again." Nostalgia had pulled him over there, the hope that if he revisited the places he'd been with Eloisa he could close the door on that chapter of his life. "The press doesn't know the reason they renewed their vows so soon after saying them in the first place. They got married to safeguard custody of my niece, my brother Kyle's daughter. Her biological mom dumped her on Phoebe, then disappeared." Anger chewed his gut all over again when he thought of how close his niece Nina had come to landing in foster care. "The whole mess really rocked our family. Thank God little Nina is safe."

"You love your niece?" she asked, her face inscrutable.

"Gotta confess, I'm a sucker for kids. I take pride in being the favorite uncle. Want to see pictures of the rug rats?"

"You carry family pictures?" she squeaked incredulously.

"Got a whole album on my iPhone." He unclipped the device from his belt and tapped the screen until pictures filled the display. He leaned closer to her. "My brother Sebastian and his wife remarried after divorcing each other. They have a son."

He brought up an image of his toddler nephew taking his first steps. Then clicked to an infant girl. "That's Sebastian and Marianna's daughter. They adopted her then her birth mother changed her mind."

He swallowed down a lump in his throat and kept his eyes averted until he could speak again. "Here's my brother Matthew—"

"The senator from South Carolina."

"Yes. This is him with his wife and their daughter at the beach." He shuffled to the next photo. "And this is a family portrait taken in Portugal. There's Mom with her husband, the General, his three kids with their spouses and children."

"Your family is huge."

Her family wasn't so small either, when taking into account her biological father and his three sons, but mentioning that didn't seem prudent. "Christmas can be rather noisy when we all get together at the family compound in Hilton Head."

"It's amazing you can gather everyone for any event with all the high-profile commitments."

"We make time for what's important." Would she see and understand that his family was about things more important than a press release or bank balance?

She leaned back in her chair, crossing her arms defensively. "Your brothers are happily married, which means your mother is probably riding your back to produce a happily-ever-after of your own with a wife and make chubby-cheeked cherubs, so you dig up me."

Not even close to what he'd intended. He placed his phone on the end table by the glass paperweight. "That's one helluva scenario to draw from a simple update on my brothers."

"You're not denying it."

He was losing ground here and he wasn't even sure why. "My mother may be a strong-willed politician in her own right, but I'm also very much her son, strong will and all. No one coerces me into anything."

"Unless that influence comes from the bottom of a bottle."

"I wasn't drunk the night we got married." He'd only had two of the local beers. "That was you."

"Are you saying you actually wanted to be married to me?"

"I thought so at the time."

Her mouth fell open, her eyes wide with horror. "You were in love with me?"

"The magnitude of your horror is positively ego deflating."

She shoved up to her feet. "You're playing with me." She walked across the room and opened a closet full of linens. "I don't appreciate your making fun of me."

The way she so easily dismissed what had happened between them a year ago really pissed him off. Okay, so their wedding had been an impulsive mistake. His brothers had been getting married. He'd had this idea that what he felt around Eloisa resembled what his brothers described about finding "the one." He may have been wrong about that. She may have had a couple of drinks, but she'd been clear about how much she wanted him, too, how much she'd needed him.

Need wasn't love. But they had felt something for each other, something strong and undeniable.

"I would never mock you." Frustration sliced through him with a razor-sharp edge. "There are far more interesting things I would like to do with you tonight. Let's back up to the part about sex."

She laughed. "At no time were we talking about sex."

"You mentioned making cherubs." Yeah, they were engaging in good old-fashioned bantering but damn, he found it arousing and a fine way to take the edge off his anger. "I'm sorry if your mother never got around to giving you the talk, but sex makes babies."

Her face closed up again. "You're not half as funny as you think you are."

"I'm halfway funny? Cool."

She dumped an armful of linens into his lap. "Make up your own bed on the sofa. I'm done here."

He watched her grab her purse before pounding up the steps to her bedroom, and he couldn't even rejoice over the fact she'd let him stay. Her door clicked shut behind her, the sound of a lock snicking a second later.

Somewhere along the line he'd misstepped. And he didn't have a clue what he'd done wrong now any more than before.

Upstairs in her room, Eloisa sunk to the edge of her bed, sliding down to the floor. She clutched her knees, tears making fast tracks down her face.

Seeing Jonah touch that glass paperweight had almost driven her to her knees earlier. After she'd lost the baby four months into her pregnancy, she'd had a private memorial service all her own for her child. She'd taken a tiny nosegay of white rosebuds to the beach and let waves carry them away as she'd prayed.

She'd kept one rose for herself. The bloom had dried far faster than her tears. Then she'd had the bud encased in glass along with a couple of tiny shells and some sand from that stretch of shoreline.

Jonah obviously loved children, evident not just from his words but from the way his eyes had gone soft over that family photo album. Each beautiful baby's face had torn a fresh hole in heart, tormenting her with what her child—hers and Jonah's—might have looked like.

The doctors had told her it was just one of those things. There was no reason why she couldn't have more children, but she couldn't see any way clear to having forever with any man, much less starting a family.

Between fears about threats from her father's enemies to even deeper fears about living out her mother's legacy... Eloisa swiped her eyes with her forearm.

God, she was mess.

What would Jonah say if he learned she'd kept the pregnancy a secret from him?

She still didn't understand why she'd delayed contacting him about the baby. She'd told herself she would let him know before their child was born. When she'd miscarried and her emotions had been such a turmoil of grief, contacting him seemed an overwhelming hurdle.

Every day that passed, it seemed easier to stay quiet. Telling him now wouldn't serve any purpose.

Her cell phone chimed from inside her purse, startling her midsob. She definitely didn't feel like speaking to anyone this late. Thank goodness the chimes indicated a text message.

She fished out her phone. Her sister's name scrolled across the screen. Eloisa thumbed View.

R U home? Worried about u.

Eloisa clutched the phone. She'd never shared her burdens with anyone before. The secrets were too big, too deep. Unburdening herself would be selfish. She stifled back the crazy notion of what it might feel like to spill her guts to her sibling.

Eloisa typed out, *Am home and ok. No worries.*

She sent the message and pushed to her feet. She needed to splash water on her eyes and go to sleep. Would that be possible with Jonah downstairs on the sofa?

Her phone chimed in her hand. Audrey again.

What about tycoon hunk? Is he there?

She set the cell on the bathroom counter next to the sink. Her fingers hovered over the keypad. What should she tell her sister?

He was most definitely bothering her by his mere presence so much more than she could have even expected. But if she wanted time to figure out what to do about him, her father, her biology, she needed to play along with his bizarre game a while longer.

Beyond that? What did she want?

Eloisa looked at herself in a mirror framed with seashells and sand dollars. She picked at a strand of hair that had slipped loose from her severe ponytail, her face devoid of makeup. But her cheeks were flushed in a way they'd never been before—except for that too-short month in Spain.

The truth settled inside her with a resounding thud. She couldn't be the sort of person who would walk into that living room, whip the covers off Jonah and say to hell with the consequences, she was making the most of her marital status. She'd gone that route before and it only led to their current mess.

A tempting alternative tickled at her brain. What if she did sleep with him again, but the next time was more about fun, with no ring? She'd let things get too serious before. That had obviously been a mistake on so many levels.

Could she forget the past and have an affair with her ex-husband?

Five

Eloisa made it through the night without a trip downstairs, although it had been rough going when she'd woken up at around four.

But finally the morning sun streaked through her reed roll-up blinds. She could leave her room without feeling she'd caved. Since it was only six-thirty, she might just get to watch him sleep, something she'd missed out on during their one night together.

She pulled on a white terry-cloth robe, securing it tight before leaving her bedroom. Halfway down the stairs she realized the sofa was empty. Well, empty other than the thin quilt straggling off the side. The pillow still bore the deep imprint of a head. Eloisa padded barefoot down the rest of the steps, her toes sinking into the carpet runner along the wood.

Where was Jonah? The spare bathroom downstairs

was silent, the door cracked open, steam still lightly fogging the mirror and a pale blue towel hung on the rack. Had he left as abruptly as he'd shown up, even after joking about wanting a final night together? Just the thought of being with him again sent a tingle along her skin, a tingle doused by the possibility he'd already left.

Her bare feet picked up speed along the hardwood floor, but the kitchen was empty, too.

"Uh-huh…" His voice drifted inside.

She spun around. The French doors were open an inch. She sagged back against the island counter and stared through to the patio. Jonah lounged in her Adirondack chair, cell phone pressed to his ear. Curiosity held her still and quiet when she probably should have done something to announce her presence, like slam a couple of cabinets open and closed.

His jean-clad legs stretched out long and so damn sexy, showcased by the morning sun. There was something hot and intimate about his bare feet and while she couldn't see his chest, his arms appeared bare as well.

Memories of making love in Spain flamed hotter in her mind after simmering below the surface all night long. She may have had a couple of drinks and lost some inhibitions, but she remembered the sex. Good sex. Amazing sex. She'd been so hungry for him as she'd torn away his shirt, popping buttons in her frenzy. His chest had captured her attention all by itself. She'd known he was muscular. The ripples under his shirt had been impossible to miss, but she hadn't been prepared for the intense definition, the unmistakable strength and power far more elemental than any money or prestige.

She'd always considered herself the cerebral sort, attracted to academic types. So it had totally knocked her off balance when she'd gone weak-kneed over a peek at Jonah's pecs.

"Right," he said to whoever was on the other end of the line. He thrust a hand through his still-damp hair, slicking it back. "I realize that cuts a week off our timeline. Go ahead and send me the new specs. I'll get back to you with an answer by the end of business today." He listened and nodded. "I can be reached at this number. Meanwhile, I'll be on the lookout for your fax."

He disconnected and didn't show signs of dialing again, apparently done with chitchatting for the moment. Any second now, he might stand and notice her. Eloisa looked around for some excuse to appear busy rather than to be eavesdropping. She snatched the empty coffeepot from the coffeemaker.

Jonah stood, stretching his arms overhead.

Her mouth went dry. His chest was everything she remembered and more. She'd forgotten about the deep tan. The honey-warm glow of his skin made her want to taste him all over.

She visually traced the cut of his six-pack lower, lower still down to…oh my…he'd left the top button of his jeans open.

No boxers.

Just a hint of a tan line.

Eloisa grabbed the counter for balance.

She tore her gaze off his bare stomach and brought it to his face. He was looking straight back at her as she stood in the kitchen, stock-still, holding on to the counter with one hand. Her other held a coffeepot dangling uselessly from between her fingers.

"Sorry, uh, Jonah," she babbled, startling into action and shoving the coffeepot under the faucet as he sauntered inside. "I didn't mean to interrupt your call."

"It's okay. We'd already wrapped up business." He tucked the phone half into his pocket, studying her as intently as she'd studied him. "Are you making coffee or tea?"

The intensity of his gaze made her edgy. Was her robe gaping? Her hair a mess?

She glanced at the pot…. Damn. She'd forgotten to turn on the faucet.

"Coffee." Eloisa turned her back to him and focused on making extra-strong java. Hopefully by the time the last drop dripped she would have scavenged some self-control and dignity. "Were you talking to your lawyer about moving forward on the divorce?"

"That was a work call." The heat of his voice and breath caressed her shoulder and she hadn't even heard him approach. He moved quietly for such a big man.

"You have a job?" she asked absently, setting the glass pot on the counter rather than risk dropping it. When had her fingers gone numb?

He flicked her ponytail forward over her shoulder. "I think I'm insulted you have to ask."

Ducking away, she opened the cabinet and foraged for her favorite hazelnut-cream-flavored beans. "Weren't you working on your grad studies like the others when we met?" She glanced back at him. "I assumed…"

He cocked an eyebrow. "You assumed that I was a perpetual student content to live off Mom and Pop's nickel? You sure painted quite a picture of me with very little info."

She finished pouring coffee beans into the coffeemaker, closed the lid and hit Start. The sound of the grinder grated along her already ragged nerves. "You made assumptions about me, too."

"Such as?" He leaned against the counter, dipping his head into her line of sight.

"I gave off the appearance of being someone different during those weeks in Madrid." She crossed her arms over her chest, keeping her robe closed and her hands off his chest. "That time of my life was very out of character for me."

"How so?"

"I'm a homebody, not a world traveler. I like my books and my Adirondack chair with a mug of coffee. That sort of exotic adventure was a onetime good deal. I lucked into a scholarship program that granted me the extra credits I needed. Bottom line, I'm a bookish librarian, not a party girl who gets drunk and impulsively marries some hot guy."

"You think I'm hot, huh?" His blue eyes twinkled as brightly as the rising sun glimmering through the sliding patio doors.

"You already know I find you physically attractive." She conjured her best "librarian" voice that put even the rowdiest of hoodlums in place. "But there are more important issues to address here."

"Of course." He selected an apple from her wicker fruit bowl on the counter. "I have a theory."

"What would that be?" They were nearly naked. He had an apple.

Where was the snake? Because she certainly was tempted.

He gestured with the fruit in his hand. "I think you *are* the sort of woman who travels the world and impulsively takes risks, even knowing sometimes those risks may not work out. Deep down you want to take more of those risks because you also know that sometimes things do work out."

"You seem to have decided a lot about me."

Without answering he crunched a big bite off the side. Why couldn't he have chosen one of the more innocent oranges or plums?

She watched his mouth work. She'd done that before, in Spain during a late-day picnic with the whole crew. Back then she'd only indulged in what-if fantasies about Jonah, never for a second thinking she would one day act on them.

And here she was daydreaming about the feel of his mouth moving along her skin...

Except his mouth was moving because he was talking and she didn't have a clue what he'd said.

"Pardon me?" She rearranged the plums until the fruit was balanced again.

He set aside his half-eaten apple. "Our time together was intense. You can learn a lot about a person in time-compressed moments."

What was he driving at? "But you agreed with me the morning after that we'd made a mistake."

"Did I?"

She stared back into his serious blue eyes and tried to understand him, understand this whole bizarre reunion. But he wasn't giving away anything in his expression. She wasn't so sure she could say the same for herself.

Eloisa touched his hand lightly. "Don't play mind games with me. I know what I heard. And it's not like you came after me."

"I'm here now."

What if he'd come after her right away? She would have told him about the baby. She wouldn't have been able to stay silent if face-to-face with him. How much different things might have been.

Or maybe not. Her mother certainly hadn't experienced a fairy-tale ending when she'd gotten pregnant.

Eloisa shook off the haze of what-ifs. "You've shown up for your one night of sex. Followed by a divorce."

"Who says we can't change our minds?" Before she could answer, he pitched his apple into the corner trash can. "I have to check on that fax."

Blinking fast, she watched him walk out the door shirtless, her head still spinning from his abrupt departure. The front door closed, but she could still see him through the skinny windows on either side of the door. The limo loomed conspicuously in the parking lot, idling alongside the curb. Jonah ducked his head and climbed inside and she remembered that mobile office/command center.

And she realized he'd never answered her question about his phone call or what he did with his life now. While Jonah seemed to have figured out so much about her, she had precious little other than Wikipedia information on him.

If she really wanted to move forward with her life, the time had come to quit drooling over the guy's body and start seriously looking at the man underneath.

* * *

He'd seen the desire in her eyes underneath her veneer of calm.

Jonah tugged on a black polo shirt while he waited for Eloisa to finish her shower upstairs. No amount of work in his fax machine could distract him from thoughts of her under the spray. In some ways he thought he remembered every nuance of her body. That night was burned in his memory.

Would his fascination with her ease if he had more time with her? He certainly hoped so because he didn't want another year like the one he'd just endured.

The sound of water faded, then ended. Silence echoed for what felt like forever before he heard the rustle of her upstairs in her bedroom. Getting dressed.

He'd never considered himself a masochist, but listening to her was serious torture. Jonah pivoted away from her door and opened cabinet after cabinet in search of a coffee mug. As he started drinking his second cup, he heard her door click and swing open.

Jonah poured some java for her, spooning two sugars in the way he remembered she preferred. And why he recalled that detail, he didn't know. He turned to face her.

He stopped short. Reality definitely beat the hell out of memories—and she wasn't even naked.

Eloisa stepped into the kitchen barefoot, wearing a simple blue sundress. The flowing lines clung subtly to her curves, and her skin glowed warm and pink from the shower. Her black hair was wet and pulled back in her signature ponytail, exposing her neck. He'd seen her arousal earlier when he'd hung up the phone and he could probably persuade her now....

But he didn't want to win in some all-out seduction. He wanted *her* to come to *him*.

Eloisa took the cup from his hand carefully, so carefully their fingers didn't even brush. "Did you get your paperwork?"

"Yes, I did." His next job didn't begin for another thirteen days. Most times, he would have headed out early. He was about to tell her about the nineteenth-century Peruvian hacienda he'd been hired to renovate and expand into a resort.

Then remembered she'd only asked because she thought he was contacting his attorney about the divorce.

She blew air across the top of the cup, watching him through upswept lashes. "I don't have much for breakfast, just some granola bars or toast and whatever's in the fruit basket. You're welcome to what's here."

If only she meant that the way he wanted her to. "I can feed myself."

"Good then." She nodded. "Tell me more about your job."

Hey, wait. "But I don't have one, remember? I'm just a lazy playboy."

She lowered her cup, genuine contrition lighting eyes as dark as her coffee. "I was wrong to make that assumption. I genuinely want to hear now."

He wasn't so sure he wanted to be in the hot seat, and definitely didn't know what had brought her to this about-face from pushing him away to shooting the breeze together. "Don't you have to get to work or help your sister with wedding plans?"

"Audrey's busy today, and I have a half hour before I have to leave for the library."

"I'll let the chauffeur know."

"No need." Turning away, she cradled her mug in both hands and walked to the sofa, her hips swaying gently, loose folds of the dress swishing a hypnotic *follow me.* "My sister's fiancé took care of returning my car. She already texted me that it's out in the parking lot."

"Then you're all set." He watched her place her coffee on the end table.

She pulled his blanket from the sofa and began to fold. "Tell me about your job."

He set his mug beside hers and reached for the end of the quilt trailing the ground. "What do you want to know?"

"Why do you hang around historic sites rather than slick new buildings?" She came closer, nearly chest to chest, and met his hands.

His eyes held hers and he considered kissing her right then and there, but he was determined for her to close that last gap. He knelt to sweep up the ends of the blanket and stood again. "I'm a history buff, always have been even when I was a kid, and my family traveled overseas a good bit."

Finishing the final fold, she clasped the quilt to her chest and sat on the sofa. "Tell me more."

She hadn't taken the chair this time and he wasn't missing the chance to get a little closer.

Jonah swept aside a couple of froufrou decorative pillows and sat beside her, keeping space between them. For now. "I'm an architect. I specialize in historic landmarks."

"That's why you were in Spain last year." She sagged back, her face relaxing into a smile for the first time since he'd seen her last night. "But you were also a student, right?"

He shifted uncomfortably. Couldn't he just give her a résumé? "I finished my dissertation."

"You completed your PhD? I'm impressed."

He winced. He hadn't shared that with her to wow her. He preferred not to talk about himself at all. "I enjoy the subject matter." He shrugged offhandedly. "I had the luxury of not worrying about school loans."

"But you were also in Spain in a more official capacity?"

"Yes, I was." What did she hope to accomplish by grilling him?

"Why did you keep it a secret?"

Was this a trap? "I didn't keep anything a secret."

He just didn't feel the need to relay everything to everyone.

"You're playing with words." She leaned closer, her shower-fresh scent, the tropical perfume of her shampoo, teasing him. "You can't blame me for making assumptions when you won't share. Well, tell me now. What else were you doing there?"

To hell with figuring out motives or playing games. He had her here. Talking to him. Not running. If he had to scavenge chitchat to make headway with her, then fine. Might as well dish up some information about his past. "When I turned eighteen, I decided I didn't want to live off my family. While I was in college, I started flipping houses."

"You worked construction in college?" She set aside the quilt and reached for her coffee.

Good. He had her relaxing bit by bit. "Is there something wrong with that?"

She paused midsip. "Of course not. I just… Okay, I made assumptions about your college years."

"I didn't have time for the frat-boy scene, princess." He'd worked his ass off, and considered the time well spent as it gave him real-world experience once he'd graduated. "So I flipped houses, made investments then took things to another level by underwriting renovations of historic manor homes and castles. I made more investments." He shrugged. "And here I am."

"What about your family's influence in world politics? What about your inheritance?"

Some of the women in his life had been sorely disappointed to hear about his lack of interest in being a part of the political world his family inhabited. "What about it?"

"Do you just leave the money sitting around?"

"Hell, no. I invest it. I expect to leave more for my kids."

"You want children?" She averted her eyes, setting her mug down.

"Damn straight, I do. A half dozen or so."

She pushed to her feet abruptly, backing away, nearly stumbling over her bare feet. Eloisa grabbed the chair for balance. "I need to finish getting ready for work."

What the hell had caused her quick turnaround? He'd been sure he was making headway and suddenly she was checking her watch, shoving on her shoes and scooping up her purse.

Maybe he'd hit a snag there by pushing too hard, too fast. But he wasn't one to admit defeat. It was all about building on the progress he'd made, one brick at a time. He watched her rush around the town house, gathering herself on her way out the door. And as she turned to wave goodbye, he realized.

She'd put on lip gloss.

He thought back to the evening before. She'd been stunning, silhouetted against the waterside, wind rippling her dress and lifting her hair. She had an unstated style and innate grace that proclaimed her timeless beauty regardless of what she wore.

And he was damn sure she hadn't worn makeup last night or a year ago. Yet for some reason, she'd slicked on gloss today. Sure, it was a minor detail, but he found himself curious about every detail surrounding the woman he'd married.

They'd made a decent start in getting to know each other better today. Although they'd mostly talked about his job. And now that he thought about it, he didn't know much about her career since she'd transitioned from being a student.

If he wanted to get closer to Eloisa, perhaps it was time to learn a little more about *her* workplace.

Six

Eloisa perched on the second-to-top step of the rolling ladder, replacing two copies of *The Scarlet Letter*. They'd been returned by a couple of high schoolers who'd lost their classroom edition and had to check it out from the library in a panic before the test. And while work usually calmed her, channeling peace through the quiet and rows of books... Today the familiar environment fell short of its normally calming effect.

She placed the blame squarely on her husband. Having Jonah show up in her life again so unexpectedly was unsettling on too many levels. No wonder she was having trouble finding her footing. She'd contacted her attorney and it appeared Jonah's claim was correct. The divorce hadn't gone through after all. Her lawyer had received the paperwork just this morning, although he vowed he had no idea how Jonah had learned of her Medina roots.

The lawyer had gone on to reassure her he would look into it further. In fact, he planned to go straight to the source and speak with her father and brothers directly. If they didn't have the information, they would need to be warned, as well.

She aligned the books and started back down the ladder. A hand clamped her calf. Gasping, she grabbed the railings to keep from pitching over backward. She looked down fast—

"Jonah," she whispered, her world righting and narrowing to just him, "you scared the hell out of me."

"Sorry about that. Wouldn't want you to fall." He kept his hand on her leg.

Eloisa continued down, his hand naturally sliding up for an inch, and another. Her heart triple-timed as she wondered how long he would keep up this game.

She descended another step.

His hand fell away. The heat of his palm remained.

Soft chitchat sounded from a couple of rows over, the air conditioner nearly as loud as the conversation. Otherwise, this section of the library was pretty much deserted this morning.

Eloisa gripped a shelf since the floor felt a little wobbly. "What are you doing here?"

"I came to take you out. Unless you have to do something with your sister's wedding plans, in which case, I'm here to supply lunch." He gripped the shelf just beside her, his body blocking the rest of the row from sight and creating a quiet—intimate—haven.

A lunch date? God, that sounded fun and wonderful

and more than a little impulsively romantic. *So* unwise if she wanted to keep her balance while finding out what made Jonah Landis tick. "I already bought a sandwich on my way in."

"Okay, then. Another time." He looked past her, then over his shoulder, a broad shoulder mouthwateringly encased in his black polo shirt. "Mind if I have a tour of the place before I leave?"

Her mouth went dry at the thought of more time with him. She eyed the water fountain. "It's a public library. As in open. To the public. Like you."

He traced down the binding of a misplaced Dickens book. "I was hoping for my own personal tour guide. I'm partial to sexy brunette librarians who wear their long hair slicked back in a ponytail. And if she had exotic brown eyes with—"

"I get the picture, you flirt." She held up her hand and stifled a laugh. "You want a tour?" She pulled *A Tale of Two Cities* from the shelf and tucked it under her arm. "Of a library?"

"I want a tour of *your* library. You saw my workplace in Spain." He propped a foot on the bottom step of the ladder. "Now I want to see yours."

Could he really be serious here? Could he perhaps, like her, need some additional insights in order to put the past behind him? The whole flirtation could just be his cover for a deeper confusion like she felt.

And she was probably overanalyzing. Didn't men say things were a lot simpler for them?

Regardless, what harm could there be in showing him around the library? She couldn't think of anywhere safer than here. Now where to start?

If she took him downstairs to the reception area, she

would face questions later from the rest of the staff. Better to go farther into the stacks.

She mentally clicked through other areas to avoid. A book-group discussion. A local artist in residence hanging her work. Eloisa discussed the facility's features by rote.

Jonah reached ahead to push open a doorway leading into a research area. "What made you decide on this career field?"

She looked around. Definitely secluded. She could talk without worrying about being overheard, but also she wouldn't have the same temptations of being alone in her town house with Jonah. "My mother spent a lot of time staying under the radar. I learned low-key at an early age. Novels were my…"

"Escape?" He gestured around the high-ceilinged space that smelled of books and air freshener.

"Entertainment." She shoved a chair under the computer desk. "Now they're my livelihood."

"What about after your mother married what's-his-name?" Jonah followed, palming her back as she rounded a corner.

"My mother still liked to keep things uncomplicated." How in the world had her mother ever fallen for a king? And a deposed king at that, with all sorts of drama surrounding his life? Enrique Medina seemed the antithesis of her stepfather, a man who might not be perfect, but at least had been a presence in her life. Loyalty spurred her to say, "His name is Harry Taylor."

"Yeah, what's-his-name."

Eloisa couldn't help grinning. Her stepfather wasn't a bad guy, if a bit pretentious and pompous…. And she knew in her heart he loved his biological daughter more than he loved her. It hurt a little to think about that, but not anywhere near as much as it used to. "While I appreciate your championing my cause, I truly can stand up for myself."

"Never doubted that for a second," Jonah answered without hesitation. "What's wrong with other folks— like me—throwing our weight in along with you?"

She simply shook her head. "I thought you wanted a tour."

"We can tour and talk."

Sometimes she wasn't sure if she could walk and chew bubblegum around this man. She plastered on a smile. "Sure we can. And here's my office."

Eloisa swept the door open wide and gestured for him to follow her into the tiny space packed full of novels, papers and framed posters from literature festivals around the world. She placed the Dickens classic on a rolling cart to be shelved later.

The door clicked as it closed. She turned to find the space suddenly seeming way smaller with Jonah taking up his fair share of the room that wasn't already occupied by her gunmetal-gray desk, shelves and an extra plastic chair for a guest.

Maybe her office just felt claustrophobic because there weren't windows or even a peephole in the door. Not because they were alone.

Totally alone.

He hadn't planned on getting her alone in the library.

Yet here they were. Just the two of them. In her tiny, isolated office.

Jonah pivoted away to find some distraction, something to talk about, and came nose to nose with a shelf of books. Art books and history books, all about Spain and Portugal. She wasn't as detached from her roots as she tried to make out.

Jonah thumbed the gold lettering along the spine of a collection of Spanish poetry. He recalled she spoke the language fluently. "Have you ever met your biological father in person?"

"Once." Her voice drifted over his shoulder, soft and a little husky. "I was about seven at the time."

"That's years after the last-known sighting of him." Jonah kept his back to her for the moment. Perhaps that would make it easier for her to share. So he continued to inventory her books.

"I don't know where we went. It felt like we took a long time, but all travel seems to take forever at that age."

He recalled well the family trips with his three brothers and his parents, everything from Disney to an Egyptian pharaoh's tomb. Their vacations would have been so different from that mother-daughter trip to see a man who barely acknowledged her existence. Sympathy kicked him in his gut. "Do you remember the mode of transportation?"

"Of course."

"Not that you're telling." He couldn't stop the grin at her spunk.

"I may not have a relationship with my father—" sounds rustled behind him, like the determined restoring of order as she moved things around on her desk "—but that doesn't mean I'm any less concerned about his safety, or the safety of my brothers."

"That's right. Medina has three sons." He clicked through what he knew about Medina from the research he'd been able to accomplish on his own—when he should have been working. But damn it all, this was important. "Did you meet them as well?"

"Two of them."

"That must have seemed strange to say the least."

"I have a half sister, remember? It's not like I don't understand being a part of a family unit." Her voice rose with every word, more than a little hurt leaking through. "I'm not some kind of freak."

He turned to face her again. Her desk was so damn neat and clean a surgeon could have performed an open-heart procedure right there. Germs wouldn't dare approach.

Jonah, however, had never been one to back down from a dare. "Your mother would have already been remarried by the time you were seven."

"And Audrey was a toddler." She clasped her hands in front of her defensively.

Her words sunk in and...holy hell. "Your mom went to see her old lover after she was married to another guy? Your stepfather must have been pissed."

"He never knew about the trip or any of the Medinas." She stood straight and tall, every bit of her royal heritage out there for him to see. She ruled. It didn't matter if she was sitting in a palace or standing in a dark, cramped, little office. She mesmerized him.

And she called to his every protective instinct at the same time. What kind of life must she have led to build defenses this thick?

"Your stepfather didn't know about any of it?" Jonah approached her carefully, wary of spooking her when she was finally opening up, but unable to stay away from her when he sensed that she could have used someone to confide in all these years. "How did she explain about your father?"

She shrugged one shoulder. "She told him the same thing she told everyone else. That my father was a fellow student, with no family, and he died in a car accident before I was born. It's not like Harry talked about my dad to anyone else. The subject just never came up for us."

Jonah skimmed his fingers over the furrows along her forehead. "Let's not discuss your stepfather. Tell me about that visit when you were seven."

Her forehead smoothed and her face relaxed into a brief flicker of a smile. "It was amazing, or rather it seemed that way to me through my childish, idealistic eyes. We all walked along the beach and collected shells. He—" she paused, clearing her throat "—uhm, my father, told me this story about a little squirrel that could travel wherever she wanted by scampering along the telephone lines. He even carried me on his shoulders when my legs got tired from walking and sang songs in Spanish."

"Those are good memories."

She deserved to have had many more of them, but he kept that opinion to himself. Better to wait and just let her talk, rather than risk her clamming up out of defensiveness.

"I know it's silly, but I still have one of the shells." She nudged a stack of already perfectly straight note slips. "I used to listen to it and imagine I could hear his voice mixed in with the sound of the ocean."

"Where is the shell now?"

"I, uh, tucked it away in one of my bookcases at home."

A home she'd decorated completely in a seashore theme. It couldn't be coincidence. He gripped her shoulders lightly. "Why don't you go see him again? You have the right to do so."

"I don't know where he is."

"But surely you have a way to get in touch with him." The soft give of her arms under his hands enticed him to pull her closer. He should take his hands off her, but he didn't. Still he wouldn't back off from delving deeper into this issue. "What about the lawyer?"

She avoided his eyes. "Let's discuss something else."

"So the lawyer is your point of contact even if the old guy never bothers to get in touch with you."

"Stop it, okay?"

She looked back at him again hard and fast. Her eyes were dark and defensive and held so much hurt he realized he would do anything, anything to make that pain go away. "Eloisa—"

"My biological father has asked to see me." She talked right over him, protesting a bit too emphatically. "More than once. I'm the one who stays away. It's just too complicated. He wrecked my mother's life and broke her heart." Her hands slid up to grip his shirt. "That's not something I can just forget about long enough to sit down for some fancy dinner with him once every five years when his conscience kicks in."

He churned over her words, searching for what she meant underneath it all. "I miss my father."

His dad had died in a car wreck when Jonah was only entering his teenage years.

"I told you I don't want to see him."

Jonah cupped her face, his thumb stroking along her aristocratic cheekbone. "I'm talking about how you miss your mother. It's tough losing a parent no matter how old you are."

Empathy softened her eyes for the first time since they'd stepped into her office. "When did your father pass away?"

"When I was in my early teens. A car crash. I used to be so jealous of my brothers because they had more time with him. Talk about ridiculous sibling rivalry." He'd always been different from them, more of a rebel. Little did they know how much it hurt when people said he would have been more focused if only his father had lived. But he refused to let what others said come between him and his family.

Family was everything.

"We almost lost our mother a few years ago when she was on a goodwill tour across Europe." The near miss had scared the hell out of him. After that, he'd knuckled down and gotten his life in order. His skin went cold from just thinking of what had almost happened to his mother. "An assassin tried to make a statement by shooting up one of her events."

"Ohmigod, I remember that." Her fists unfurled in his shirt and her hands smoothed out the wrinkles in soothing circles. "It must have been horrible for you. I seem to recall that some of her family was there…. You saw it all happen?"

"I'm not asking for sympathy." He clasped her wrists and stilled her hands. She might mean her touch to be comforting, but it was rapidly becoming a serious turn-on. "I'm only trying to say I understand how you feel. But, Eloisa, once you're in the spotlight, there's no way to step back out."

"I completely get your point," she said emphatically. "That's why I've kept a low profile."

He brought her hands together, their hands clasped as he tried to make her understand. "You were born into this. There's no low profile. Only delaying the inevitable. Better to embrace it on your own terms."

"That's not your call to make," she snapped, pulling her hands away.

God, it was like banging his head against bricks getting this stubborn woman to consider anything other than a paradigm constructed a helluva long time ago. "Are you so sure about your father's reasons for choosing to close himself away?"

Her spine starched straight again, ire sparking flecks of black in her eyes. "What are you hoping to accomplish here?"

He'd been hoping to learn more about her in an effort to seduce her and had ended up pissing her off. But he couldn't back down. "You don't have to play this their way anymore, Eloisa. Decide what you want rather than letting them haul you along."

Her hands fisted. "Why does this need to get so complicated, and what the hell does it have to do with you?"

Anger stirred in his gut. "I'm the guy who's still married to you because it's so complicated. Damn it, Eloisa, Can you understand my need to do something, fix this somehow?"

"Maybe there's nothing to fix. And even if there is, do you know what I really want?"

"Okay. Mea culpa." He thumped his chest. "You've got me there. I haven't got a clue what you want from me."

"Well, prepare to find out." She clasped his face in her hands, only giving him a second's warning.

Eloisa planted her mouth on his.

He blinked in shock—for all of three seconds before he hauled her against him and kissed her right back.

As her arms slid around his neck, he decided the time had come to take this as far as she would go.

Seven

Eloisa couldn't decide if she'd just made the best or worst decision of her life. Regardless, she knew she'd made the inevitable choice in kissing Jonah. They'd been leading up to this from the second he'd stepped out of his limousine last night.

She pressed her body closer to his, fully, for the first time in a year, her mouth opening to welcome him. Last night's staged kiss outside the party had been too brief. She'd somehow forgotten how well they fit, the way she tucked just inside his embrace, his head angling down. He was taller than she was, but somehow it worked just right for her arms to rest on his shoulders while she burrowed her hands into his hair.

And ohmigod, his hair.

Eloisa touched and roved and savored his head, the slight waves curving around her fingers as if coaxing her to stay. No persuasion needed, she was on fire with want after a year without this kind of sensual contact.

She'd reached for him in frustration, her desire slipping past when her defenses were weakened by irritation. But now that he was touching her, stroking her, coaxing her body against his, she forced all that ire away, just put the whole argument right out of her mind.

Still, part of her feared he'd sparked something deeper inside just by caring enough to ask the hard questions others avoided. He confronted things she liked to keep tucked away.

Either way, she didn't want to argue. She wanted that connection she remembered from a year ago, and she didn't want to fight it another second.

"You taste like apples."

"My lip gloss," she gasped.

"Ah," he said, smiling against her mouth. "You're wearing lip gloss today." He traced her lips with his tongue, then dipped deeper, sharing the hint of flavor with her.

His kiss growing bolder, fuller, he backed her against the desk and she welcomed the bolstering because she wasn't sure how much longer her legs would hold. Jonah stroked her back, her sides, the tops of her thighs, nowhere overtly intimate but intensely arousing all the same. His hot breath caressed her neck a second before his mouth skimmed her oversensitive flesh. Her spot. *He remembered.* The fact that he still knew what she liked turned her inside out as much as the touch of his lips to her skin.

She bit back a moan, her head falling to rest on his shoulder. "We need to slow this down. I'm at work."

He pressed a finger to her lips, still paying detailed attention to her neck. "Shhh. We're in a library. Haven't you ever made out in the library?"

"Never," she answered, one word all she could manage.

"Or caught people making out in the stacks?" His hands slid up and down her sides, each time grazing farther and farther over her ribs, just below her breasts.

"A time or two." She'd sent them on their way like a good, responsible adult, but right now she was feeling anything but responsible.

Jonah nudged his leg between hers, the thick press of his muscled thigh sending sparks of pleasure radiating upward. And clearly she wasn't the only one feeling the effects of their clench. There was no mistaking the rigid press of his arousal against her stomach. He wanted her. Here. Now.

And heaven help her, she wanted him too and to hell with the emotional fallout later. Hadn't she thought just this morning about how wonderful it would be to indulge with Jonah, no marriage, no strings? And other than a piece of paper, they weren't really married. Their lives wouldn't be tangled up beyond these next couple of weeks.

"Let's continue this at my house." She took the leap. "Or at your place even."

"Trust me. I wouldn't risk getting you in trouble." He kissed her quiet again.

They had their clothes on. She was off the clock for lunch. He was only kissing her.

Kissing her senseless.

But still. Who could object? When she'd stumbled

upon other couples necking in the library before, while it had been mildly embarrassing for the people caught, all had just laughed good-naturedly. And she was locked in her office on her lunch break.

Why not?

"Okay then, I trust you," she vowed against his mouth, meaning the words for now, this moment.

"That's what I want to hear." A smile kicked up into his cheek as he lowered his head to hers.

She threaded her fingers through his hair again. Thick and luxurious, wild and sexy. Like the man.

Jonah angled her closer. His palms spanning low on her back, he urged her into a gentle rock against him. His leg pressed more firmly. Pleasure tightened more insistently. She ached for release but held back, nervous and excited by the notion of losing control. They were just making out, for heaven's sake.

Memories of a similar embrace in his rented home in Spain steamed through her mind, of him pressing her just this way against the kitchen counter when they'd made a 3:00 a.m. forage for food. Naked. Both of them had been exhausted and starving from their workout in bed. The images of then tangled with the present until the clothed kiss became so much more in her mind.... She could almost smell the sangria and fruit juices they'd licked from each other's bodies.

It had been so long, too long, a whole damn year without this feeling, a growing sense of frenzy no man other than Jonah had been able to engender. What if he were the only man who could stoke her passion to this level? What would it be like to go through life never feeling this level of want and pleasure and pure sensuality again?

The warm sweep of his tongue, the familiar taste of him, stoked her need higher, hotter, tighter. She wriggled to get closer. The tension gathered low, right where he so perfectly teased. He pressed his leg more insistently against, rocking it rhythmically against her until she realized...

Gasped...

Couldn't stop...

He caught her moan with his mouth. She arched her back, flinging full-out into her release. Every muscle inside her pulled taut as if to hold on to the sensation as long as possible, clenching up each sparkling aftershock.

Slowly, the warm flush along her skin began to cool. She shivered and he gathered her against his chest. Thank God he didn't speak. She would have been mortified, but she could barely think, much less talk.

Jonah brushed his mouth along the top of her hair. "Enjoy the rest of the lunch break and your sandwich. I'll pick you up for supper."

Then he was gone. The door to her office closed behind him with a gentle swoosh while she sagged into her chair. Eloisa smoothed a shaky hand over her hair, to her lips, against her still-racing heart.

She didn't regret her decision, but had to admit, she'd been so very wrong. Things with Jonah could never be uncomplicated. She'd just had the best orgasm of her life.

And he'd only kissed her.

He'd only kissed her.

Parked in her town house lot five hours later, Jonah shut off the engine on his rental car—top-of-the-line

Range Rover, the same sort he always picked and owned because it worked best for him on work sites.

He'd spent the afternoon settling into Pensacola a little deeper, renting wheels. He'd stopped by his penthouse suite to complete paperwork and calls, also lining up two of his employees to oversee the early work trickling in unexpectedly.

Basically, he'd spent the afternoon figuring out ways to make his schedule more open to Eloisa. Damn, how his brothers would laugh at him if they were here to see, but he refused to lose this chance to settle things with Eloisa.

With the scent of her still all around him, he knew he wasn't giving up. He had to have her.

Jonah draped his wrist over the steering wheel and stared at her door. Their encounter in the library had gone just as he'd planned…and yet it hadn't turned out at all the way he'd imagined.

No way in hell could he have imagined being this rocked by seeing her come undone in his arms. This was moving so fast and if he wasn't careful, she would bolt again.

Good thing he'd made reservations at a restaurant. He wasn't sure he could withstand another evening alone with her in her place.

He reached for the car door and his cell phone chimed, stopping him short. He unclipped it from his waistband. His mother's number from her airplane phone scrolled across the screen.

It still blew him away that diplomats and politicians around the world feared his mother's steely nature. Ginger Landis was tough, sure, but she was also fair with a soft heart.

He thumbed the Talk button and turned on the speaker phone. "Hey Mom, what's up?"

Jonah cranked up the Range Rover again so the A/C would keep the car cool on the muggy May afternoon.

"Just checking in on your schedule." Computer keys clicked in the background. Ginger was undoubtedly working while talking, the phone tucked to her ear, holding back her signature grey-blond bob that always stayed as in control as she did. His mom took multitasking to a whole new level: ambassador, wife, mom to four children and three stepchildren and known as a superwoman to boot. "I'm finishing up a summit in Washington. I'll be back in South America before you arrive in Peru for your next project. I'm looking forward to living near my youngest son, even if it's for a short time."

"Me, too." The Landises all spent so much time on the road with their careers, family visits were valued all the more. And while he had his ambassador mother's ear. "Hey, do you have any inside-track info on the deposed king of San Rinaldo?"

She hesitated for a beat before answering. "Why would you ask that?"

"Rumor has it, he's in Argentina." And his mom just happened to be ambassador to a small neighboring country.

"That's the word around town."

He knew his mother would never break security rules, but if she could just point him in the right direction…. "Officially or unofficially?"

"Honestly, I don't know the answer either way," Ginger said, her voice even tighter. He thought of it as her office voice. "Jonah, I can say that there is a compound in Argentina built like a fortress. There's a lot of activity going on inside and very little coming out. Either he's living there, or he's done a good job of creating a red herring."

"Medina has the money to accomplish that."

She laughed lightly. "That, I most definitely can confirm. The old king built a fortune beyond the royal inheritance. The estate continues to multiply itself. We know he has three sons—Carlos, Duarte and Antonio."

And he had a daughter, a daughter no one knew about. Eloisa, so unforgettable and deserving of so much better than she'd gotten from the people who were supposed to care about her.

And what about how *he* had treated her? Damn it all, Eloisa deserved to have someone a hundred percent on her side. "Thanks, Mom. I would appreciate it if you could ask around—quietly, please—about the Medinas."

"Certainly, I'll see what I can find." Curiosity slipped ever so subtly into her voice. "Would you like to tell me why?"

Eloisa's secrets weren't his to share. But the time would certainly come when his family would have to learn he'd married her. The fact that he'd hidden it for the past year was going to piss them off enough. "Is that a requisite to your help?"

"Of course not," she said, backing off smoothly. "I'll let you know if I discover anything soon. Otherwise, I'll see you in a couple of weeks."

"Looking forward to it. And hey, Mom? Love you."

"I love you, too, Jonah," she said softly before disconnecting.

Perhaps talking to his mom had heightened his conscience or maybe he'd just woken up. But regardless, he needed to shower Eloisa with romance as well as sensual enticement. He couldn't be sure how this was going to turn out. But he wasn't walking away or letting her walk away until he was damn sure everything was out in the open and resolved.

Jonah rang the doorbell and waited…and waited. No answer. Eloisa had told him she would be home around this time, but wasn't answering her phone or cell. His instincts burned. Something was off.

She'd given him a key and he intended to use it.

He opened the front door and pushed inside fast. "Eloisa? Are you home?"

His heart slugged his rib cage harder with each step as he searched her empty town house. Then he thought about her patio. The curtains were closed over the French doors. She must be outside relaxing.

He opened the doors to the patio and sure enough the chair was full. But the person most definitely wasn't Eloisa, or even a female.

Jonah scrubbed a hand over his jaw to mask his surprise and figure out what to do about this intruder who looked completely at home. As if he belonged in that chair, at Eloisa's place.

Jealousy cranked into high gear as he summed up his opponent.

A large male sat in the Adirondack chair—dark haired, about six foot three inches. The guy appeared toned, but Jonah had a few pounds on him. He just needed to decide what move to make next.

At first the guy's eyes seemed closed, but when Jonah

studied him further, he could see the man watching ever so carefully through narrow slits.

This guy was ready to pounce.

Jonah blocked the exit. "What the hell are you doing on Eloisa's patio?"

His eyes opened slowly, a haughty smile not far behind. "I've come to visit my sister."

Eight

Well, that took care of the jealousy.

Jonah stared at the guy in front of him claiming to be Eloisa's brother. How could he trust this dude was on the up and up? But then perhaps he was someone who'd just ended up on the wrong patio. After all, the stranger had simply said he was visiting his sister, no name given.

"Who did you say you're looking for?" Jonah asked.

The man smoothed the front of his dark suit jacket—no tie on his white shirt open at the collar. "Where is Eloisa? My sister. Our family lawyer informed us she has concerns. I came right away."

First, he needed to determine if this man could be trusted. Sure, he looked like he could be Eloisa's brother, same dark hair and brown eyes. The aristocratic air was there, too, but his skin was more olive toned.

Because both of his parents were from the Spanish region?

Still, he needed to go on the assumption that this guy knew nothing about Eloisa, that he could be some reporter searching for information...or worse.

Jonah shut the door to the town house and stepped closer to the looming guy in a dark suit. "And your name is?"

He thrust out his hand, lean and ringless, no jewelry other than a pricey watch peeking from his cuff. "I am Duarte. Hello, Jonah Landis."

Jonah jolted. How did the man know him? Sure his family name was easily recognized, but it wasn't like his face was familiar to the average Joe—or in this case, Duarte. "How did you get in here?"

"I jumped the fence."

This guy in a suit hopped fences? Odd, and not the sort of behavior he expected from a prince.

Still the fence apparently posed a security problem he would be addressing shortly. "Do you make a habit of that? Jumping fences? Breaking and entering?"

Duarte—or whoever the hell he was—arched a single brow slowly. "I would have come through the door but she is not here."

"Eloisa doesn't have any brothers. Just a sister named Audrey."

Duarte simply smiled. "Eloisa can clear this up soon enough. And as you noticed, I already know who you are, and I know how you are connected to my sister." He frowned slightly. "I guess that makes us brothers."

Jonah braced his feet, shocked that Eloisa would have

revealed their marriage to anyone, but she said she didn't talk to her family, only communicated through a lawyer. How had this guy found out? And was he even who he claimed to be?

This joker wasn't getting past him. "How about you leave a calling card?"

"Good, good." He nodded curtly. "I like it that she has you to protect her."

That threw him off-balance for a second. The last thing he'd expected was acceptance, encouragement even.

Except he knew better than to be swayed by calculated words. "What did you say you're doing here?"

"I've come to see Eloisa for our father. And you're wise not to trust me. That's best for her."

While they may have found a point of agreement, that didn't mean Jonah intended to back off pushing for whatever he could get out of Duarte. "Where does your father live?"

"Ah, you're tricky, not ever saying the last name either, never giving anything away. Your questions and answers are as nebulous as my own." He gestured toward the French doors. "Let's go inside. Less chance of being overheard."

"I don't think so. Until I hear from Eloisa that you're welcome, we can stay right here."

Duarte glanced around at the small fenced-in patio, vines growing up the wood, a small fountain in the corner with a cement conch shell pouring water into a collection pool.

And only one chair.

Duarte nodded regally. "We will stand here, then, until she returns."

Jonah leaned on the doorframe with affected nonchalance, every muscle still on high alert as he watched the man for any signs of aggression or deception. "So step out on a limb and spill your guts for me."

The strange guy threw his head back and laughed. Finally, he shook his head and quieted. "I travel everywhere. But our father? He can no longer travel anywhere because of his health, and he wants to see his children. You don't have to confirm anything I say. I don't expect you to."

"Dude, I'm thinking it's time to call the cops and arrest you for trespassing."

"I could give you all sorts of identification, but you know that IDs can be purchased. Instead I will tell you a story about the last visit Eloisa made to see her biological family when she was seven—I was seventeen. We all went on a picnic, then walked down the beach. We collected shells. Then Eloisa rode on our father's shoulders while he told her a story about a princess squirrel who could travel anywhere she wanted, anytime."

Damn. This guy could really be…

"Then he sang her songs in Spanish. Does that answer your questions?"

"You've definitely captured my interest enough to delay calling the cops." He might not know everything about Eloisa, but he was certain she would blow a gasket if her family news was splashed all over a police blotter where any newspaper could snatch the scoop.

"I'm not worried."

"You're a cocky bastard."

"Thank you." He slid a finger along his shirt collar,

the first sign that he felt the heat or any tension. "I'm not only here because Eloisa called the lawyer. I am also here because our father is sick."

"Your dad, the guy who sings lullabies in Spanish? How sick is he?"

"I am not the kind to predict worst-case scenarios. Let's just say he's very ill. A visit is in order before the opportunity is lost forever."

How would Eloisa take hearing Enrique Medina could die…or was already dead and she'd missed seeing him? He'd encouraged her to make contact with the old king if for no other reason that to settle the past, and now the clock was ticking. If this man could help persuade her, all the better. And with Jonah by her side, nobody would stand a chance at hurting her ever again.

In fact, there should be some apologizing and amends for needing such a dire prod to make this offer.

"Even if I might think it's in her personal best interest to see him, why should Eloisa—or any woman—visit a family you say she hasn't seen since she was seven? If that's all true, perhaps they should have tried harder to contact Eloisa more often over the years." The silence stretched between them, birds chirping, cars roaring and honking in the distance, even the ocean echoed distantly. "What? No disagreement?"

"Why would I argue when you're absolutely right? That doesn't mean Eloisa could live with doing the wrong thing now."

Jonah checked his watch. Where the hell was Eloisa? She should have been home twenty minutes ago. "Your family is exempt from the rules but she's not? She's supposed to do the right thing regardless? That's bull."

"She is a part of our family."

"Says you. I'm still not sure what you're talking about."

"It's her choice to live this way rather than claim her birthright." He tipped his head to the side. "You didn't know that? She and her mother chose a long time ago not to accept anything from him. He slipped help how he could. Surprise prize winnings, bonuses at work, even a fellowship to travel to Europe."

Eloisa would spit nails if she found out the whole trip was a setup. But given her prickly ways about money, that would have been the only way to get her to accept anything. "Most women I know wouldn't like being manipulated that way."

"Then don't tell her."

"Why are you telling me?" That put him in a tough position, forcing him to keep secrets. He hated lies. Always had. His father had hammered that into his head from a young age. His dad had been in the military before he'd gone into politics. He'd prided himself on being a rarity—a guy who shot straight from the hip, no matter what.

He'd always said the measure of a man was how he acted when no one was looking.

"I am hoping you can hold some sway over her to see my father for what may very well be the last time. She needs persuading. She's a stubborn woman."

"Wait. Hold on for just a damn minute. You say you haven't seen her, but you know all about her personality?"

He shrugged. Did this dude ever relay any emotion? "I never said we haven't kept close watch over her."

She definitely wouldn't like that. Even if this guy

was on the up and up, another possibility still existed. He might be a stalker. Family could stalk. And dealing with that possibility took precedence. "It's time for you and me to leave."

"You and I?"

"I'm not letting you walk away until I am one hundred percent sure who you are. I have connections of my own."

"Fair enough. Just one question first." Duarte's dark eyes narrowed as if zeroing in for the kill. "Who did you think I was when you entered?"

The sound of a key rattling in the front door jarred the silence between them. Damn it all. He should have moved faster. The hinges creaked and Jonah put himself between this man and the path Eloisa would take.

Eloisa filled the open French doors, two grocery bags in her arms and her mouth open wide.

"Duarte?"

Shock nailed her feet to the floor.

Eloisa blinked fast twice, unable to believe her eyes. It couldn't possibly be one of the Medina brothers.... Did he even go by Medina?

But she'd seen a few pictures over the years and she would never forget the faces of her faraway brothers. That summer she'd visited, Duarte had told her of his dream to take a new last name, maybe his mother's maiden name, and move out of the compound, into the world. Duarte had been emphatic about making his own way in the world.

She'd understood that, even at seven, when he'd talked about his plans for "getting the hell off this island."

Island? Until just this moment she'd forgotten that part of talking with him.

From his slick suit, gold watch and some kind of signature cologne, it didn't seem he'd done too badly for himself. She was glad for him if he'd managed to fulfill those dreams of leading his own life.

Although he had managed to send all her evening plans up into smoke.

Eloisa juggled bags of groceries in her arms as her purse dangled from her elbow. She would have set them on the counter when she'd entered the apartment, but she'd heard two voices on the patio and rushed out there, food and all.

She'd traded a favor at work and clocked out early. She was always the one staying late for others who had surprise dates.

It was fun to be on the other side of that for a change. So much for fun.

Both men stepped forward to take a sack from her arms, the food she'd bought with such grand ideas for her evening. She'd taken great care in making her selections at the market. Deciding had been tougher than she expected because what could you serve a tycoon world traveler?

She'd opted for a simple regional classic that might actually have a chance at being heavy enough for a big guy like Jonah—shrimp and grits, with slaw and biscuits on the side. She'd splurged on a bottle of good wine. Well, what she considered good, which could very well be swill by his standards. Not that it mattered now since they had an extra guest.

Her hands shook with nerves and she nearly dropped

her purse. How silly to be this uptight about making dinner for a guy.

Dinner for her husband.

She felt the smile on her face before she ever realized she'd reacted. Seeing him made her happy. Wow. What an awesome—and scary—notion.

Especially with this huge distraction between them. Before she could do anything, she needed to find out why her brother had shown up here so unexpectedly.

The space between them might be short—the patio was microscopic, after all—but there might as well have been a mile between them. Hugging this distant man she'd only spoken to once seemed awkward, even if they shared the same DNA.

And now that she thought about, how strange for him to be here. A trickle of unease tickled inside her stomach. "Come into the town house, gentlemen. Let's get those groceries inside before the shrimp spoils in this heat."

Eloisa flashed a grateful smile to Jonah. She couldn't miss the tic in the corner of his eye, but wasn't sure what put it there.

"Duarte," she touched her brother's arm lightly, "welcome. You might as well stay for supper. Unless you've already made other plans?"

Once in the kitchenette, Jonah's somber gaze stopped her midramble. "Your brother said he needs to talk to you."

"Right, of course. We have a lot to catch up on, I'm sure." God, this felt so surreal, having her brother here after so many years.

She put away groceries on autopilot. Holding a wrapped and taped bag of shrimp in her hands, she pivoted toward the refrigerator and almost slammed smack into her brother. "Sorry, uhm, not much space."

"How did you recognize me?" Duarte asked simply, with no preamble.

She looked into dark eyes identical to her own, ones that had also stared back at her from her father's face during that memorable encounter years ago. "You look just like him."

"Our father?" Duarte blinked slowly, his eyes more enigmatic than their dad's. The old king's eyes had been mostly sad. "You were only seven years old."

"But Enrique was younger then." Although in her childish view he'd seem so very ancient. "And my mother kept a picture of him from when they, uh, knew each other. She let me hide it in my sock drawer sometimes. I mixed it in with fan clippings and posters so no one would ever guess. And it's obvious I'm right."

She couldn't bear this standoff positioning. Eloisa strode past to shove the bag of seafood into the refrigerator. She had to be in control of something, even if it was making sure the shrimp didn't spoil. "Why are you here? Now?" Eloisa froze as a horrible possibility avalanched over her, far more chilling than the blast from the fridge. She spun back around. "Is he dead?"

"He's alive," Duarte reassured her quickly, even though his somber face gave her pause. "I'm here because you contacted the lawyer. And we would have been in touch with you soon anyway. Our father is sick, most likely dying. He wants to see his children."

"How many of us are there?" Damn, where had that cruel response come from? From the deep recesses of her late-night childhood fears and tears, no doubt.

Jonah placed a comforting, steadying hand between

her shoulder blades, while nudging the refrigerator closed with his foot.

Duarte stuffed his hands in his pants pockets. "Just you, our two brothers and, of course, me."

"Pardon me if I'm not so sure." Eloisa breathed deeply to expand the tightness rapidly constricting her rib cage with tension. "I am sorry he's sick, but I don't think we have anything to say to one another. Not after so many years."

She expected an argument, smooth persuasive reasons why she was wrong. But Duarte simply shrugged.

"Okay then. I'll let him know the message was delivered and you declined. Since you don't have any questions, I've completed my task."

That was it? He was leaving?

Duarte slid a card onto the sofa end table, simple white vellum with a number printed in raised, black ink. He anchored it with a paperweight. "You can contact me when you decide to see him."

When?

Another decade or two?

Duarte had simply shown up, rocked her balance until she didn't know what she thought, and then he was gone again before she could gather her thoughts. He hadn't come to *see* her. He'd come to pass along information. God, she was such an idiot, still hiding hopes deep in her heart like those pictures of her biological family tucked under her socks.

She wanted to cry but her eyes were dry after all these years.

Jonah stepped around her, nearly nose to nose with her brother. "I'll walk you to the door."

"No need." Duarte nodded to Eloisa, starting toward

the front door. "I'll let our father know you will be visiting soon."

She stifled the urge to scream out her frustration. Who did these Medina men think they were to blast into a person's life once every decade or so and wreak total havoc? "You're assuming a lot."

He pivoted back toward her fluidly. "There are many times when my life has relied on my ability to read people."

Duarte Medina slipped out of the door as quietly and quickly as he'd arrived.

Jonah rubbed between her shoulder blades. "Are you all right?"

"I'm fine. Totally fine. Why wouldn't I be? It was just five minutes out of my life. No big deal. Now he's gone and everything's back to normal again." She pulled away and yanked open the refrigerator. "I'll start supper."

His hands landed on her shoulders, squeezing gently with a sympathy and comfort that swept away her defenses. She shattered inside from endless vows that she didn't care if her father never fought for her. And when her brothers struck out on their own, they never even bothered to contact her. Years of being everyone's support and nobody's princess crashed down on her until she hurt so bad inside she couldn't find any corner of her soul to hide and escape.

She had nowhere to go except straight into Jonah's arms.

Nine

Eloisa blocked out the ache in her heart left from her brother's shocking visit and focused on Jonah. Just Jonah, with her, both of them hopefully naked very, very soon.

She wrapped her arms around his neck and flattened herself to him. He stumbled back a step and nearly slammed into the kitchen counter.

"Whoa." He gripped her hips, steadying them both so they didn't knock off the remaining groceries or tumble to the tile floor. "Let's slow this down a minute and think things through. I know you're upset—"

"Damn straight, I'm upset. I'm angry and hurt and confused and want it all to go away. You can fix that for me, so let's get to it."

She plastered her lips to his, opened, demanded. The ever-ready attraction between them blazed to life on contact, thank goodness. She welcomed the blissful sensation expanding within her, pushing everything else to the far corners. Less pain.

Total pleasure.

Muscles in his chest and arms twitched and flexed under her searching fingers. "Eloisa, I hear you and I understand. And God knows, I'm more than glad to comply until you're not able to think or talk, but I also have to know you're not going to bolt out of here afterward before I even have time to pull on a pair of boxers."

Eloisa nuzzled along his ear, kissing, nipping, whispering soft gusts of air over his skin as she buried her face in his hair. "We're in my home. That makes leaving a lot tougher for me."

"But not impossible," he insisted even as his hand slid down to cup her bottom and lift her closer, more intimately against him until she could feel the fly on his jeans straining against the thickening length of him.

"We're here to resolve things," he said, "not make them more complicated between——" He clasped her hand already making fast work of his jeans snap. "Take a breather, for now, anyway."

She flipped her hands to link in his as she met his eyes square on. "Jonah, look around you. Think. What did I bring in when I got home from work? Dinner. Wine. I planned a romantic meal because after what we did——" she paused, suddenly breathless at just the mention, the memory "——after the way you made me feel, I've been thinking about finishing this every second since. I've been planning what I want to do to you, how to make you every bit as crazy as you make me."

"Eloisa," he groaned, loosening his hold on her hands

until she flattened her palm to his fly. "You already make me crazy just by walking through my mind, much less the room."

"Then it's time to do something about that."

She peeled his black polo shirt over his head. Was it only last night he pulled up at her sister's party? It seemed like a lifetime ago, as if the past year apart hadn't even happened.

But it had and oh God, she couldn't let herself think about that. Better to focus on now, with him. He was right. They did need time together to work through their feelings or she—he too?—would spend forever wondering, wanting.

Growling low, he tunneled his hands under her dress, bunching it up and away in a deft sweep that left her breathless and bare, other than her icy-blue lace bra and panties. "Do you have any idea how gorgeous you look right this second?" He reached behind her to pull the scarf from her ponytail, releasing her hair. "I've lost a lot of sleep this past year thinking about you like this."

"I hope you're going to lose even more tonight." Her hair teased along her skin until she was ready to scream for a more insistent touch.

Thank goodness he didn't need any further encouragement. He kissed her again, backing her as he moved forward, their legs tangling in the desperate dance toward the stairs, which stopped them short.

But not for long.

Jonah ducked his shoulder into her midsection and lifted her into a fireman carry. Eloisa squealed, but certainly wasn't about to tell him no because he was making fast tracks for her bedroom.

Once in her room, he flipped her over and onto the

antique bed with a smooth sweep, the wooden thrift store find she'd painstakingly whitewashed. She bounced once in the middle of the pouffy comforter. A pink tulip print hung over the headboard.

Her haven where no one entered.

Until Jonah.

He traced her collarbone. "When I watched you sleep before, I fantasized about what kind of jewels would look best nestled right here." He skimmed his mouth along after his fingers' path.

"And here." He nipped her ears.

"I didn't think I slept," she gasped as his mouth trekked lower, "for even a minute that night."

"I didn't need more than a minute to picture you in my world."

Her breath caught as his words sunk in. Her eyes met his, so deeply somber for a second, then he smiled and she lost the chance to decipher what she'd seen.

"Besides," he said, shuffling away the seriousness, "I have an active imagination." He traced her belly button with his tongue, flicking her simple silver ring between his teeth. "Most definitely a diamond here."

Jonah kissed her hip, his hand sliding down her leg and scattering thoughts as quickly as the rest of his clothes and their underwear. "And anklets. There are so many options for stones I would have specially set for you to wear right there for trips to the beach."

A ceiling fan clicked, gusting over her bare skin and ruffling airy sheers that hung from bamboo rods. She felt like those curtains, fluttering and writhing with every brush and breath of Jonah's along her body. She grasped at his back, his taut buttocks, his chest, touching and tasting frenetically in contrast to his smooth exploration.

How could she be this hungry for Jonah when by all rights, he had taken care of her needs just a few hours before in her office? That should have at least eased the edge, but instead seemed to have only made her ache for more. Then he slid up along her, over her, the solid weight of him anchoring her to the bed and the moment so perfectly.

She slid the arch of her foot along his leg, opening for him, wanting him, welcoming him inch by thick, delicious inch.

"Shhh..." he whispered in her ear although she couldn't for the life of her remember what she'd said or asked for. "Patience. We'll get there."

Unable to wait, she slid her hand between them and clasped him, caressed him, coaxed him until his hands shook, too. He reached to the floor, to his pants, his hand returning with a condom. He tore open the packet and sheathed himself before she had time to do more than be grateful one of them was thinking clearly enough to take care of birth control.

Finally, he was inside her again, the pressure of him familiar and new at the same time, but then Jonah had always been an unpredictable mass of contradictions that shuffled her perfectly ordered world.

Braced on his elbows, he stared down at her, holding her with his vivid blue eyes. His jaw, tight with restraint, told her he ached for this as much as she did. She'd been tipsy when they'd been together before, but this time she was stone-cold sober, aware of every moment and sensation. And it was even better. Her senses were heightened, sharp, *responsive*.

He moved over her while the bed rocked under her. He was so large and gentle, completely focused on her and...oh my, what a heady feeling that was after so long in shadows. She wanted to stay right here and bask in the sparks showering through her, but knew there was no way in hell this could last. Maybe next time... There had to be a next time.

Frantic to hold on to the feelings, to him, she clenched around him.

"Eloisa..." His eyes closed, his jaw clamping tighter as he said her name again and again, telling her exactly how often he'd thought of her, the other ways he dreamed of adorning her in jewels, erotic images and possibilities she'd never considered and now couldn't forget.

She tried to answer, but words... She had nothing except a moan of increasing need. Jonah's hands fisted in the pillow on either side of her head, his head dropping to rest on her brow.

His hair slid forward, covering most of his face. She cupped his cheeks, her fingers playing with the wavy strands and wondered if he'd ever considered letting it grow longer. Somehow it seemed more lord of manor, leader of the land, with its extra length. He was the epitome of fairy-tale fantasies she'd only barely dared acknowledge to herself.

More, she wanted more of him, of this, of the whole fantasy. She hooked her heels behind his back and arched upward, accepting him deeper. Her fingernails scored desperate furrows down his back as the intensity gripped her, begging for release. This couldn't last much longer. It was too intense. Too much of everything and already the ending built and tightened and tingled through her in ripples she couldn't hold back any longer....

She didn't bother trying to hold back the shout of pleasure. Jonah thrust faster. She gripped his back harder. Sparks glinted behind her eyes much like the jewels he'd detailed earlier. With one last prolonged thrust, he buried himself inside her...and stayed, his face in her hair, his groan against her ear until his arms gave way and he rolled to his back, taking her, replete, alongside him.

His hand slid over her stomach, his finger tracing a circle around her belly button, his breathing ragged. "We're definitely going shopping for a diamond soon."

Her heartbeat tumbled over itself at the mention of diamonds...until she realized he meant navel rings, not engagement. Technically, they were already married anyway. But for how long?

Jonah continued to draw lazy circles with the backs of his fingers. A murmur of unease echoed inside her as she thought of their baby that had rested there, tragically too briefly. She should tell him, and she would, but how could she just toss it into the mix right now? More importantly, how could she trust he would stay? He'd made it clear he'd been angry with her for leaving. She couldn't help but wonder if he'd come looking for revenge.

Could he be that calculated? She had no way of knowing because as she'd told him before, they didn't know each other well enough to be certain of anything. Her best bet? Wait—a couple of days, perhaps?—to let the dust settle. To let her mind clear while she got her bearings. Then she would tell him about the baby they'd lost.

As the fan dried the perspiration on her body, she

wondered how long she could selfishly take from him before the truth put this tenuous connection to the test.

Reclining in Eloisa's antique bed, Jonah tested a lock of her hair between his fingers, so long and soft. He'd wanted to have her and walk away. He'd expected to put an end to their unfinished business by being with her one last time, and instead? He couldn't imagine how the hell he would let her go.

If they weren't married, he would have asked her to travel with him. Why not ask her anyway? Certainly they couldn't solve anything continents apart.

He knew her secret now, after all. Sure, being with him brought an added level of attention, but her heritage could too easily come out no matter what in an unexpected instant. Better to be prepared.

He was the man who could keep her safe.

Now he had to persuade her to go with him to Peru after her sister's wedding. And wouldn't waking up beside Eloisa daily be a pleasure? Not that he expected her to agree right away. She was stubborn, and she had a blind loyalty to her sister and stepfather that made him grind his teeth in frustration.

He needed to show her the way their lives could blend, that she deserved better from people. He cared about her in a way her self-absorbed family never had.

Jonah took in the every curve draped in a cotton sheet, a light purple. She looked damn good in that color. Natural purple diamonds were among the rarest. Like her. But he intended to shower her with jewels *and* his undivided attention.

He released the strand over her breast where it curled

to rest around the creamy swell. "I've missed you so damn much this year."

"We barely knew each other then." She rasped a fingernail lightly down his chest. "And things are happening so fast again now. Can't we just enjoy this moment?"

"Think how much we've learned in just a day of really talking. Let's talk some more." He splayed his hand over her rib cage, then upward to toy with a pert nipple. "I've missed being with you, seeing you, feeling you move underneath as you whisper how much you need me, need more of what I can give you."

She laughed, covering his mouth with her hand. "Okay, okay. I get the picture."

He nipped her finger, then drew it in to soothe away the sting with his tongue. "You can't tell me you never thought about those days together."

"Of course I thought about it." The sheets rustled as she sat up, hugging her knees to her chest. "You have a way of making an impression on a person that isn't easy to forget. Staying away was my only option for keeping my sanity."

"I make you crazy? Good." He swept her hair forward over her shoulder and traced down her neck to her spine, one vertebrae at a time. "Let's see if I can do it again."

"You know you do, on so many levels." Sighing, she rested her cheek on her knees as he made his way down her back.

"Then let's *talk* some more."

"I'm still finding my footing. I'm not exactly the tumultuous type, you know. Let's deal with the most basic level for starters."

"You've got a one-track mind right now." And while he sure as hell wasn't going to complain about that, he also noticed the way she wouldn't meet his gaze. Not a good sign.

She smiled, still not looking at him, instead inching the sheet ever so slowly off him. "What's so wrong with a married couple having sex? Lots of sex. In every room and vehicle at our disposal. We can talk the whole time. In fact, I've already got a pretty good idea of some things I'd like to say to you, too."

He clasped her wrist, stopping her, holding her until finally she met his gaze. "I'm being serious here, Eloisa. We shared something special just now. We'd be fools to just toss that away again. But for it to work, I need you to be honest with me this time."

Eloisa clutched a pillow to her stomach, the shadows and pain so intense in her eyes he wanted to scrap the whole conversation and just hold her. What in the world could have hurt her so deeply? He started to ask, but she pressed her fingertips to his mouth.

"Jonah, I hear what you're saying, and while I joke about all that married sex, honestly, in my mind—" she tapped her temple "—we're divorced. We have been for a long while. It's going to take time before I can reconcile all these changes. So much is happening so fast…I want to trust it…trust you."

"Then do it."

"That's easy for you to say. You're adventurous by nature." She eased her wrist free then clasped his hand. "Just this—" she raised their linked fingers "—is risky for me."

"I don't believe that, not after the woman I met a year ago." He paused, realizing, holy hell, she really was scared. There was a side to her he hadn't met in Spain. He honestly didn't know the woman he'd married. And if he intended to stand a chance with her now, he needed to push harder than he had before.

He had to understand her in order to keep her. He searched for the best place to start. "Are you upset about your brother showing up tonight? Hearing your father is ill had to be upsetting. Are you going to see him? Is that what's wrong?"

She looked down at the bedspread for so long he wondered if she would answer. Would she decide to cut him off at the knees? He wouldn't be pushed aside again without seeing this through.

"Eloisa?" He tipped her chin up with a knuckle. "I asked about your father."

"My father...right...uh, I haven't decided." Her grip eased on the hugged pillow. "I don't even know what to think about Duarte showing up here. It was so unexpected, I'll have to give this more thought."

"But you believed him when he said your father is ill." He sat up beside her, stroking her hair back from her face.

She didn't flinch away.

"My lawyer does keep me informed to a certain degree. I know what my brothers look like. They were already teenagers when I saw them before. Even if I don't know where everyone lives." She laughed dryly. "Actually I don't want to know. Being responsible for their safety would be too scary."

He didn't like the way they left her out here, unprotected. Then it hit him that he couldn't let her go. *He* couldn't leave her out here unprotected. There weren't many who could protect her at the level she needed.

But he was a Landis.

And even though there had been times he'd bucked the Landis conventions, right now he welcomed every bit of power the Landis influence could bring if it kept Eloisa from being hurt in any way—physically or emotionally—by her Medina ties.

The Landis influence and money could also bring her peace in other ways, pampering that by rights should have been hers from the start. "You need a distraction."

"You've done a mighty fine job of that tonight." Looping an arm over his shoulders, she leaned against him, kissing him with unmistakable promise.

His pulse jackhammered in his chest, throbbing through his veins thicker, lower, urging him to act now. He steadied his breathing and his resolve.

Stick to the plan. More time with her. Show her how well she could fit in his world, how easily she could leave her old one behind. "I'll up the ante. You took the afternoon off. Any chance you can call in sick for a couple of days?"

Interest lit in her eyes, followed by wariness. "I have to help Audrey."

"When's her next shindig?"

"Joey's family is throwing a party—" a tentative hope replaced the wariness on her face "—but it isn't until the weekend."

"So that's not a problem for you as long as you come back. Can she handle her own plans for two days?"

"I could take care of things by phone." Her words

tumbled over each other faster. "The bridesmaids' fittings are already done."

"That just leaves your job at the library. Can you get time off?"

"There are people who owe me favors." Her slow seductive smile turned him inside out. "It depends on what you have to offer."

"Trust me," he urged her, determined to make that happen on every level. "You won't be disappointed."

Ten

"Open your eyes."

Late afternoon nipping her arms with prickly heat, Eloisa pulled Jonah's hands from her face and gasped in awe. She stood on top of a building overlooking a massive canyon sprawled out in a craggy display of orange, brown and bronze rock. Wind tore at her clothes with an ends-of-the-earth force. She inched to the edge, grasped the scrolled iron railing and found she stood on top of a mammoth hacienda-style retreat, built on the edge of a cliff corner.

When they'd left Pensacola earlier this afternoon, Jonah had kept the windows closed on the airplane and the limo windows had been shaded. By their fourth hour traveling she was nearing the edge of her trust factor, but wow, had her patience ever paid off.

The property was deserted. Scaffolding remained

visible on one side of the expansive resort building, though no workers filled the platform levels of it today, their work apparently complete for the week. The historic hacienda appeared to have had a recent makeover, the scent of fresh paint mingling with the light fragrance of a potted crepe myrtle nearby.

She leaned farther over the rail. Terra-cotta pots were strategically placed around the patio with a variety of cacti—prickly pear, blooming hedgehog, spiking organ pipe, saguaro, even a towering Joshua tree. Below, in a stomach-lurching drop, away from the sculpted rooftop garden, cacti dotted the landscape in sparse and erratic abandon, no less beautiful. "This is magnificent. Where exactly are we?"

An eagle banked into a dive—*down, down, down*—so far it seemed impossible to continue, then it swooped upward again into the purple-blue sky. Warm sun counteracted the dry breeze pinning her cotton halter dress to her skin.

"Does it matter where we are?" He dismissed the luxurious digs around them and pointed outward. "Can't it be beautiful just because it is, rather than because it has a fancy pedigree attached?"

She snorted on a laugh. "Spoken like a savvy investor who can see the possibilities in previously unappreciated properties."

He clapped a palm over his chest. "I'm wounded you would think I'm so calculating."

"You're practical, and I admire that." In fact, the more she learned about him the more she realized how she'd stereotyped him from the start. "You're not at all the reckless playboy I mistook you for last year."

"Don't go romanticizing me. I simply found a

job that suits my wandering feet and desire to create luxurious digs."

She started to laugh, then stopped to look beyond his casual dismissal of her compliment. "I think it's more than that for you."

"Maybe. I'm a guy. I don't analyze like you women. I just know that I like transforming things others have overlooked." He smiled distractedly before his eyes cleared again. "We're in West Texas, by the way. I figured that was about as far as I could go without you freaking out over the secrecy or worrying about getting back for your sister's party."

"You guessed right." She accepted his conversational shift for now since he actually had shared more than she expected. "I'm glad I took the leap of faith and joined you."

Thank goodness Audrey hadn't been upset by the prospect of her leaving for a few days. In fact, Eloisa had been surprised at how readily her sister had encouraged her to go away. Only a week ago, Audrey had been hyperventilating over punch flavors, insisting she needed Eloisa and the caterer's input on everything. Brides were notoriously edgy. She could understand and be patient.

Yet suddenly Audrey seemed calm. Go figure.

Regardless, that seemed a universe away now. She'd packed so carefully for this trip, choosing her most silky underwear, remembering to pack cologne, and her favorite apple lip gloss he'd so intensely—deliciously—noted in the library. Just this morning she'd even spied him sniffing the tube at her dressing table.

Yes, she'd taken care in choosing what to bring along, cautiously pinning high hopes on this outing.

She wanted reassurance they had a chance at a future before she could open herself up to him totally. This compressed time together, away from distractions offered that opportunity.

She trailed her fingers along the curved railing. "So this place is your work? I'm very impressed."

She couldn't miss his artistry as she looked down at the structure built in such a way she couldn't distinguish the old from the new.

"The resort is set to open in another month once the decorators have finished their gig inside. Working this place landed me a contract in Peru to pull off something similar with a nineteenth-century structure. It'll need expansion as well as renovation." He shook his head. "Enough about work. We're here to relax, alone up here where no one can see us and no one will dare interrupt. Now it's time for the real reason I brought you."

Jonah turned her to the right along the corner for even more canyon panorama and, just to her side…

Rippling water slipped off the edge of the building, somehow disappearing. She pivoted to find a rooftop pool, but unlike any she'd ever seen before. It stretched off the end of the building and seemed to blend into the horizon.

"Jonah?"

"It's an infinity pool," he announced.

It was magnificent. "Infinity pool. That makes sense in theory—" given the way it blended into the canyon view "—but I don't understand how."

Her feet drew her closer to the clear waters swirling over the blue tiles, sunlight sparkling diamondlike dots along the surface. The romanticism reached to her heart already softened by a night spent in Jonah's arms.

Even now, she could feel her body reacting to just his presence, the knowledge that she could have him right now and indulge herself in everything he had to offer. And he did offer her so very much on so many levels.

Eloisa reached for his hand, listening to his explanation and letting herself dream. Maybe, just maybe her instincts had been right that all they needed was more time.

Jonah linked his fingers more firmly in hers. "The pool is architecturally designed with the edge smoothed out until it seems to extend forever, blending into the horizon. Some call it a negative edge. A side is built slightly lower with a catch basin that pumps water back into the pool."

"That sounds extremely complicated." She didn't have to be an architect to tell this required incredible talent and expertise. She imagined the least miscalculation during construction could crumble the cliff. Much like the delicate balance and attention to detail needed in building a relationship. "Tell me more."

"An infinity pool can be built on a rooftop or into the side of a mountain or right against a larger body of water." He stretched a hand toward the horizon. "The effect is the same. While you float and stare out, boundaries disappear."

"Possibilities are limitless." That sounded good in theory, but felt scary for a woman who found comfort and safety in the cool confines of her dimly lit library stacks. She would take it one deep breath at a time, because the thought of turning back scared her even more than standing here at the precipice.

His arm dropped to his side. "There's an infinity pool in Hong Kong on the roof of a hotel that's the most amazing thing I've ever seen." He squeezed her fingers. "Wanna go?"

"What? Now?" Startled by his abrupt offer, she backed away a step, instinctively craving the safety of even a few inches away from wide-open abandon. "We just got to Texas. I'm still soaking everything in."

"But you want to go."

Did she? Could she just drop everything at his whim and see the world?

"I think so, maybe," she said to the adventure. To him. This didn't seem the place for stark realities and secrets. It was the ultimate place to lose yourself. Here, she didn't have to worry about what it meant to be a Medina or a Landis. "For a short time perhaps, but—"

"Quit thinking about afterward. Enjoy the now, here at the edge of a canyon. Take a risk, librarian lady."

She bristled instinctively. "Who says there's anything wrong with being a librarian in Pensacola, Florida?"

He tugged her closer to him, his hand soothing along her waist. "I never said there was anything wrong with your profession. I'm just offering you the chance to *experience* the books. You can have it all."

Stark realities intruded all the same, memories of her mother, memories of her own, even glimpses of her father's pain-filled eyes. Consequences for stepping out of her safety zone could be huge. "They killed my father's wife, you know. They assassinated her while trying to get to him." She looked into his eyes for answers, for reassurance. "Doesn't your family worry about that kind of lurking threat? Your father may have died in a car wreck, but you had to be aware of danger at an early age."

God knows, she had worried for her mother. And in

the darkest, quietest times of night, she even worried for herself.

The wind lifted Jonah's hair and flapped the edges of his sports coat. "I hear you, and yes, my family has lived with the reality of possible kidnappings and bribes and threats because of political stands. It's not fair, but that's how things are even if we gave away the money and left the public scene tomorrow. No one would believe we didn't have something hidden somewhere. The influence remains and we have a responsibility to use it wisely." He cupped her face in his sun-warmed hands. "You can't live your life dictated by fears."

She pulled out of his arms. Leaning against, leaning *on* him would be too easy.

"Tell that to Enrique Medina." Her chest went tight. How much longer did her father have left? "He's spent nearly three decades hidden away from the world, living out his life."

"If I knew where he was, I would tell him face-to-face."

"I thought you would have learned that when you found me." Maybe she'd hoped he knew so she wouldn't have to make the choice to search. Jonah would know, blindfold her and take her there. And only now did she realize she'd hoped he would do just that today. Good Lord, she was a coward.

"Medina keeps his secrets well."

"I guess he does." As did his daughter. Guilt pinched over what she should explain to Jonah.

He drew her to his side again. "What do you think he wants to talk to you about?"

"I have absolutely no idea. Probably just to say goodbye, which I should probably go along with. It sounds simple enough. Except I have this sense that if I step into his world, I will have made an irrevocable change." She blinked back tears until they welled back up inside her soul. She tipped her head up to look at him. "Jonah, we should talk."

He thumbed under her eye, swiping away dampness that must have leaked anyway. "I think we've done enough talking for one day."

She wanted to agree, reminding herself of her resolve to wait until she was sure he would stay before risking the pain that would come from sharing all. Still, her conscience whispered. "Seriously, Jonah, I need to tell you—"

"Seriously, stop arguing. We can talk about whatever you want later." He slid his other arm around her and pulled her flush against him again, rekindling the desire that had been barely banked all afternoon. "Right now, I want to make love with you in this pool while we look out at infinity."

Infinity.

Forever.

They could have it all. She could have the time to tell him the things that needed explaining. The possibilities truly seemed as limitless of the edge of that pool reclaiming and holding everything in an endless cycle.

Jonah kissed her and she allowed herself to hope.

Jonah hauled Eloisa closer, sensing something shifting inside her, tension flowing from her in a tide as tangible as the infinity pool streaming away. He didn't know what exactly brought about the change, but he wasn't one to argue when it brought her warm and willing into his arms.

"Inside," she whispered, "to your suite."

"Here," he answered. "We're alone. No one can see us, of that I'm certain. I designed this patio with complete privacy in mind."

Over the past few months, he'd tortured himself with fantasies of bringing her up here and baring her body to the sun. "Do you trust me?"

"I can't think of anything more exciting than making love to you out here in the open." Her arms slid around his neck, her fingers in his hair. "I want to trust you."

He noticed wanting to trust wasn't the same as giving trust, but still a step in the right direction. And since he had her in his arms, ready to have sex outdoors? No way in hell did he intend to dwell on semantics.

Eloisa slid his sports coat from his shoulders, his shirt open at the collar, no tie to bother with removing. Backing him toward the double lounger beside the pool, she toyed with one button at a time, unveiling his chest until the shirt whipped behind him in the wind.

Smiling, Jonah shook his head no and danced her toward the pool instead. Her eyes widened momentarily before she grinned in return. Eloisa kicked off her sandals and trailed a toe in the water.

Her sigh of pleasure left him throbbing against his zipper damn near painfully. But soon…so soon…

He toyed with the tie behind her neck holding her halter dress in place. A simple tug set it free and falling away to reveal her breasts to the sun. He nudged the fabric down around and past her waist to pool at her feet. She kicked it away behind her, their clothes littering the stone tiles, lifting on the wind and catching on the furniture.

Eloisa glanced over her shoulder with a flicker of concern. He guided her face back toward him again. "To hell with the clothes. We brought suitcases. I'll buy you more."

"In that case…" She unbuckled his belt, slipped it free and flung it out into the canyon, with a *flick* and a *snap*.

Her uninhibited laughter rode the wind along with the rest of their clothes and his shoes until they stood bare in the open together. Her breasts brushed his chest as she took him in her hand and stroked until he worked to keep his feet steady under him.

He clasped her wrist and draped her arm back over his shoulder. Leaning, he scooped her up against his chest and started down the stone steps, the sun-warmed water churning around his legs, his hips, around his waist and higher until he slid her to her feet again. The light waves lapped around her shoulders and she leaned into him with buoyancy.

He slid his hand between her legs, the essence of her arousal mixing with the water, leaving her slick to his touch. He tucked two fingers into her warm silken grip, stroking inside, his thumb teasing outside. Sighing, she pressed closer to him just as she'd done in the library, so hot, so responsive. So damn perfect he almost came undone from just the feel of her on his hand.

She sprinkled frenetic kisses over his face, working her way to his ear. "I want you inside me, totally, I want it all here. Now," she demanded.

"More than willing to accommodate," he growled.

Jonah cupped her bottom and lifted. She wrapped her

slick wet legs around his waist, the core of her pressing closer to him, her damp heat against him. He throbbed from wanting to be inside her again. And again. How often would be enough?

She slid down on the length of him.

"Birth control," he groaned into her ear. Only now did he realize they'd forgotten and he wanted to kick himself off the damn cliff for being so reckless with her. He never, never forgot. He always protected.

Her arms clamped tighter around him. "I'm on the Pill."

"You didn't mention that when we were together before."

"My thoughts aren't always clear around you, especially when we're naked. Now can we stop with the talking and move on to the fun part? I want this—I want you. How convenient for us both that you happen to be my husband, after all."

But she hadn't known that for the past months when they'd both assumed their divorce had gone through. He didn't want to know why she'd used it in the year they were apart. He chose instead to focus on how glad to have that last concern taken away so he could...

Plunge inside her.

Her head flung back, her wet hair floating behind her. He dipped his head to take the pink pert tip of her breast in his mouth. He teased her with his tongue, gently with his teeth, using his mouth in all the ways he wanted to touch her but couldn't since he held her, guided her.

The cool jet of water from the side of the pool didn't so much as take an edge off the heat pumping through him. Water sluiced between them as they writhed against each other. Her hair floated behind her, long and dark. Beads of water clung to her face, her shoulders. He sipped from her skin, the taste of her overriding any chlorination.

He palmed her upright until her head rested on his shoulder. "I want you to see."

To look out at the endless view, the endless possibilities *he* could give her.

Eloisa gripped his arms, her nails furrowing into his skin. He welcomed the tender bite into his flesh, the tangible sign that she felt the same frenetic need.

Water lapped around them, encircling them in a vortex as he clasped her closer. He had to make this last. He refused to lose her. While they'd made progress today, still he sensed her reservations. Whatever was holding her back, he needed to reassure her she didn't have to be afraid, because he could take care of her.

He *would* take care of her, sensually, physically and any other way she needed.

The primal drive to make her his clawed through him, intensified by the open elements. He'd come here for her and found it tapped into something inside himself he hadn't anticipated. Something basic and undeniable. He thrust inside her as her hips rolled against him, her breath hitching against his neck, faster as her skin began to flush with…

Gasping, she flung her head back again, her back arching, her eyes closed tight. He watched and savored every moment of her sweet release across her face, echoed in the spasms of her moist clamp around him, drawn out until…hell, couldn't hold back.

He surged inside her. The sunset shot purple, pink and orange spiking through the horizon as sharp and deep as the pleasure blasting through him. She was his, damn it. No more barriers, boundaries, secrets.

He'd won her.

Eleven

Eloisa surrendered to the languid weightlessness of floating in the water and watching the stars overhead. How blessedly freeing to put the world and worries on hold for once. She wasn't a wife, a sister, a daughter.

Today, tonight, she was simply a woman and a lover.

After Jonah had brought her to such intense completion while she stared over the infinity pool edge, they'd held on to each other for…well…she didn't know how long. At some point she'd floated away and he'd begun swimming lazy laps. They were simply coexisting in the water without talking. Being together so perfectly, even in silence, surpassed anything she'd imagined gaining from this time away.

The near-silent sluice of his arms through the water announced his presence a second before he passed. She reached out, grazing him with her fingers. His head slid from the water and he stood beside her, not even panting.

He shook his head, swiping back his hair. "Are you ready to go in? There's a cold supper waiting in the refrigerator."

She looped an arm around his neck and let her feet sink. "It's getting late. I just don't want this day to end."

"We're not even close to finished."

Scooping an arm behind her legs, Jonah pulled her to his chest again, carrying her dripping wet into the shallow end, up the stone stairs just as he'd brought her in earlier. Rivulets of water slid along her skin, caressing, then cooling in the early evening air. Her breasts pulled tight and she couldn't miss the way his gaze lingered appreciatively.

This new ease with each other was as thrilling as his hands on her body, but also a little frightening. She pulled her focus in on the moment, on these stolen days she'd promised herself.

He cleared the last step and walked under the covered porch, elbowing open double doors to a penthouse suite. The hacienda décor reminded her of the Old World Spanish manor home Jonah had rented a year ago. Was this simply the style he was drawn to naturally, or had he somehow been as caught up in their time together as she had been?

Bold tapestries hung on the goldenrod-colored walls. She bypassed surveying all else for later. Right now, her focus stayed on the king-sized bed, definitely a reproduction of the carved walnut headboard from the room they'd shared in Madrid. Linen was draped from the boxed frame overhead, wafting in the wind from the open doors.

He set her on the thick layers of cream, tan and burnt sienna, piped in red. On her back, she inched up the bed, soaking up the amazing view of muscled, naked Jonah against the backdrop of the pool blending into the horizon. He ducked into the bathroom and came back with two fluffy towels. Jonah passed one to her and began toweling his wet hair with the other.

Eloisa knew her own sopping locks would take eons to dry out so she turbaned the soaked mass. He pitched aside his towel and gave his head a quick shaggy shake before settling beside her on the pile of feather pillows.

Tracing lazy circles on his bare chest, she stared out the open double doors, the fresh air swirling the scent of Jonah and a hint of chlorination she would forever find arousing. "I can't believe the awesome sense of privacy here."

"That's something I work to achieve with any of my projects—" his hand settled on her hip, curving to a perfect fit "—seclusion, even if there are multiple units in the resort."

"You learned the value of privacy growing up in the public eye."

"To a degree." He slid an arm behind his head, his eyes focused on the faraway. "My parents did their best to shield us, make sure we didn't feel wealthy or different."

"They sound wonderful. You're lucky to have had parents like that."

"I know." He shifted uncomfortably, then smiled as

if to lighten the mood. "And if I ever forget, my mother will most definitely remind me."

She nudged her toes against his foot. "You must have been an adventurous child, looking for new territories to explore."

"I may have given my folks a heart palpitation or two." He trapped her foot between his.

"Today, I most certainly benefited from your adventurous spirit. Thank you." She stretched upward to kiss him, not long or intense, just holding and enjoying the contact for the sake of simply kissing, even if it wouldn't go further. Yet. She tucked back against his chest. "I never even dreamed of making love on a beach, much less something like this. The fear that someone could stumble upon us, rob us, even worse..."

She shivered and wished she could have attributed it to the wind kicking in faster as night set.

Jonah unfolded a downy throw blanket draped along the end of the bed, pulling it up to their waists. "You have to know I would never put you at risk."

Eloisa snuggled closer. "Not intentionally, no."

"Not ever." He stroked her shoulders. "You're tensing up again. Stop it."

She stifled a laugh at the notion he thought he could fix anything, even the state of her muscles...and then she realized she had relaxed again after all.

"There you go." Jonah trailed his fingers down her spine. "That's more like it."

"It must be the sound of the water echoing in through the canyon, the closeness to nature at its most soothing and stark all at once. How could anyone stay tense?"

"So you like making love outdoors? I'm totally

on board with that. We could do this in any number of countries while I work restoration projects."

Her stomach backflipped. "Like showing me another infinity pool in Hong Kong?"

"Exactly. The possibilities are as limitless as the horizon."

It sounded exciting…and aimless for her. "I couldn't live my life that, just following you around the world." She pressed her fingers to his lips. "Don't even say it."

"Say what?"

"Something smug about—" she lowered her voice to mimic his "—having sex in different countries is a fabulous goal."

A tic started in the corner of his eye. "There you go again with negative assumptions about me. I can't help but wonder if you're using that excuse because you're nervous about what happened out there between us. You know damn well I have a job, a goal."

With an exasperated sigh, he plowed his fingers through his hair. "Every time I start falling for your down-to-earth strength and your passionate nature, you withdraw. Why?"

He was right, and it stung. Still she wondered, "You have a job, but how would I fit in with your plan? I need a purpose of my own."

That silenced him for the first time. She waited through at least a dozen clicks of the ceiling fan overhead and was almost ready to crack, to apologize so they could take a few steps back.

Her cell phone rang from inside her purse. He must have placed it in the room along with their refrigerated meal they'd never gotten around to eating. Not that it mattered in the least to her how it got there. She was just grateful for the distraction.

Eloisa tugged the cover with her as she stumbled from the bed for her bag resting on the trunk at the foot of the bed.

The display screen scrolled "UNKNOWN."

Averting her eyes from Jonah's obvious irritation, she thumbed the Talk button. "Hello?"

"Eloisa? This is your father."

Her stomach pitched at just the word "father" even though she recognized the voice—Harry Taylor, her step-dad. She was just too on edge since Duarte's surprise visit. "What do you need, Harry?"

She said his name in answer to Jonah's questioning look.

"It's about Audrey," Harry barked with unmistakable frustration.

Her stomach flipped faster. What could possibly be so wrong? Why had she let Jonah persuade her into running away? She should have known better than to leave when her sister was in such a fragile state. "Is she okay? Was she in an accident or something?"

Jonah sat up straighter, leaning closer and resting his hand on her back. His steady presence bolstered her as she gripped the phone and waited for her step-dad's reply.

"Audrey eloped with Joey."

Her sister had done what? Eloisa could barely wrap her brain around the very last thing she'd expected to hear.

"Oh…uh…" She struggled for words and could only come up with, "Oh."

"I can't believe she would act so impulsively, so

thoughtlessly after all I've done to make the perfect wedding for her, to give my daughter the social send off she always wanted."

Eloisa bit back the urge to note it was the send off *Harry* wanted. "I'm sorry about all the money you lost on down payments."

"You don't understand the worst of it," Harry rambled, the frustration in his voice rapidly turning to anger. "She says she and Joey are moving away, cutting ties to start fresh away from his family. She's going to throw away all the influence of his family name."

It sounded to her like her sister had wised up. Now that the shock was beginning to fade, she knew that Audrey was better off.

Jonah gave her a questioning look.

She held up a hand and spoke into the phone. "It's for the best Audrey gets her life in order now rather than risk a messy divorce later."

And didn't that hit a little close to home?

Harry's laugh hitched on a half sob. "Eloisa? Where are you? How soon can you get back, because I really need your help right now."

"Uh, I went out for a drive." And a flight. And a swim. Followed by a resounding realization that she and Jonah had very different expectations from life. While she'd more than enjoyed the peaceful aftermath of their lovemaking, she couldn't spend her entire life just floating alongside Jonah. "Don't worry, Harry. I'll be home as soon as I can."

She disconnected the phone.

Infinity had an end after all.

* * *

Jonah tugged on jeans and a button down, slicking his still-wet hair back.

God, things had gone south with Eloisa so fast.

Her family snapped their fingers and she was ready to run to their side. On the one hand, that could be an admirable trait. As a Landis, he would behave the same way in a crisis. When his brother's military plane had gone done in Afghanistan, the family had all pulled together to hold each other up until Kyle was found safely.

When Sebastian and his wife Marianna separated after their adopted daughter was reclaimed by her biological mother, the brothers had sat together through that first hellish night and poured drinks for Sebastian.

He could go on and on with the list.

Then why was he so damn irritated over this? Because no one was there for *her.* Yet they expected her to drop everything for manufactured crises that seemed a daily occurrence in Eloisa's household.

Jonah watched her yank on a fresh sundress and wished he could have enjoyed the moment more. But she was packing. Leaving. Determined to return home immediately to do heaven only knew what. Her sister had left and married some other guy. It was a done deal.

But still, Eloisa was tossing her clothes into her little bag a lot faster than she'd put them in there in the first place. What was really going on here?

Eloisa looked up sharply. "I thought you said we were alone?"

He stopped buttoning his shirt halfway up and looked around, listened. The elevator rumbled softly, then louder, closer. "Decorating staff is downstairs, but there's no reason for them to come up here, and they don't have an elevator key for the penthouse anyway."

A ding sounded just outside the suite.

His muscles tensed protectively. He checked to make sure she was dressed on his way out into the sitting area. "I said no one would bother us. Apparently I was wrong."

And he damn well wasn't happy about the interruption.

He opened the door into the hall just as a carefully coiffed woman stepped out of the private elevator. He would know those sweater sets and pearls paired with perfectly pressed jeans anywhere.

His mother, of all people, had arrived in the middle of nowhere just when he happened to be with Eloisa. His mother's arrival was too convenient. She must know something or at least sense something. He could swear his mom had some kind of special maternal radar.

Could this day go to crap any faster?

Closing the door to the penthouse quietly to seal off Eloisa from the catastrophe in the making, Jonah swore softly as he stepped toward the elevator. "Hi, Ma."

Ginger Landis Renshaw swatted his arm even as she hugged him. "Is that any way to welcome your mother? You may have gotten taller than me by the time you turned thirteen, but you will still watch the language, young man."

His mother was all protocol out in the political world, but with her family she still kept things real—even though she was now an ambassador to a small South American country.

He glanced over his shoulder at the closed door. He

could only keep Eloisa under wraps for so long. His best hope was to head off his mom long enough to go back into the suite and warn Eloisa. Prepare her for the meeting. Most women he dated either froze up around his family, or worse. They kissed up.

He was certain Eloisa wouldn't be the latter, but he worried about the former. And she sure as hell was more than a "date."

At least his brothers weren't here. "Mom, I have someone with me. This really isn't a convenient time."

"I know. Why do you think I'm here? I want to meet this Eloisa for myself rather than keep waiting for you to get around to it."

Nobody got jack by Ginger. The only question that remained? How much did she know? A lot, apparently, if she'd already learned Eloisa's name.

The door to the suite opened. His window to prepare anybody was over.

"Jonah," Eloisa called softly. "I'm packed and ready to leave, but if you're busy with work I can call a cab." She pulled up short at the sight of his famous mother. "Excuse me, ma'am."

"Eloisa, this is my mother," he said, although it seemed no introductions were needed, "Ginger Landis Renshaw."

His mother pushed past him, her eyes both sharp and welcoming. "Call me, Ginger, please. All those names are too much of a mouthful. It's nice to meet you, Eloisa."

"And you, too, ma'am," she said simply, taking his mother's hand lightly.

No shaking in her shoes.

Thus far she seemed to be silently holding her

ground and letting Ginger fill the silence with a running monologue about her trip out. Eloisa had a quiet elegance about her, a way of smoothing over even awkward situations. It was easy to see why she was the rock of her family, why both her fathers needed her by their sides right now.

God, she was mesmerizing.

"Jonah? Jonah!" his mother called.

"Huh?" Brilliant response. He peeled his eyes off Eloisa. "Uh, what did you say, Ma?"

Ginger smiled knowingly before answering. "I was just telling your delightful friend Eloisa how I had a stopover in the area to meet with a congressman friend of mine. Since I was in the States, I gave my other boys a call so we could all meet up here for a family overnight vacation."

What the— "My brothers? Are here?"

"Downstairs checking out your latest work. It's all quite lovely dear."

Apparently the evening *could* get worse.

Eloisa stepped back, as if dodging the brewing family conspiracy. "Jonah, it sounds like you and your mother have a lot to talk about. I'll just call to check in with my father while you meet with your family." She nodded toward Ginger. "It was lovely meeting you, ma'am."

She disappeared back into the suite before he could stop her. Although he appreciated the chance to find out what was up with his mother's surprise visit.

"Mom, what are you really doing here? No way in hell were you and Matthew and Sebastian *and* Kyle just in the neighborhood."

"Language." She swatted his arms again and tugged

him into the elevator. "Let's talk in here where it's more private."

"Did the General come along, too?" He could sense the family closing ranks. Something was up. And as much as he wanted to go comfort Eloisa, he needed to make sure she wasn't walking into some kind of ambush.

God, he'd thought Eloisa was quick to answer the call of her kin. The Landises could round up relatives faster than most people could put dinner on the table.

"Hank couldn't make it back from his meeting in Germany in time. He sends his best." The doors swooshed closed.

"Mom, this is nuts." And part of the reason he needed to travel. Frequently.

"This is being a mother. I can hear it in your voice when something's wrong. It's a mother's instinct, a gift I have for all of my children." She nailed the Stop button. "You asked about the Medinas and so I tapped into some resources. I found out quite a lot as a matter of fact, most of it about you and Eloisa."

Okay, she'd definitely captured his interest. For Eloisa's sake, he needed to find out every bit of information his mother had been able to unearth. "What did you learn?"

His mother pinned him with a stare she'd perfected on all four of her boys. "That you're married. And I decided that since you've been married for a year now, if I wanted to ever meet this new daughter-in-law of mine, I had better take matters into my own hands."

Twelve

Stunned, Jonah stared at his mother and processed her bombshell, along with all the repercussions it could have for Eloisa. How had his mom found out about his marriage…? "Sebastian."

Ginger nodded slowly. "I went to him with some questions when I started looking into the Medinas. He thought I already knew."

Their mother always had been good about pulling information out of them unawares. He couldn't even be mad at his brother.

Jonah pulled his thoughts back to the present. Things were still so unsure with Eloisa he needed to tread warily. "Mom, I understand your impatience, but I need for you to hold back just a little while longer." As much as he loved his family, Eloisa was his primary focus. What else had Ginger found out? "What were you able to uncover about the Medinas? Did you learn anything about the old king?"

She leaned back on the mirrored wall silently and chewed the tip of her glasses dangling on a chain around her neck.

"How much do you know about Eloisa?" he pressed again.

Ginger dropped her glasses back to rest on the chain. "I know who her real father is. A carefully kept secret for over twenty-five years, a secret that seems to be leaking out since your marriage, otherwise I never should have been able to uncover her identity."

He went stone-cold inside. He'd never for a second considered he'd put her at risk by marrying her. But of course he hadn't known her secret then. What a convoluted mess.

One he would fix. "No one will ever harm a hair on her head."

"You're that far gone, are you?" Her face creased with a deep and genuine smile. "Congratulations, Jonah."

Far gone? Hell yeah. "I'm married to her, aren't I?"

"There are problems, obviously, or you wouldn't have spent the year apart." She held up a manicured finger. "I'm not trying to pry. Only commenting on the obvious. Of course, I don't know her, but I would imagine she has reason to be wary."

"Eloisa freaks out about being in the spotlight." He glanced at the closed doors, thinking of her on the other side waiting with her suitcase. "When the time comes, this needs to be handled with a carefully worded press release."

"That's all well and good, but I meant she's wary

of being a part of a family. I obviously don't know her personally, but what I have learned makes me sad for her, and also gives me some thoughts on the subject of why you two haven't been enjoying marital bliss for the past year."

"We were doing okay a few hours ago until all the families started calling and showing up."

"Oh, really? Didn't look that way to me."

His gut churned over the fact Eloisa might have already phoned for a cab or made God only knew what arrangements while he was talking to his mom. He couldn't let her up and leave when he was distracted again, and how could he ever hope for a relationship with a woman he couldn't count on to stand still for more than a few hours at a time?

"Son, you've been blessed with family traditions so it seems simple to you. Not so much to others. Like Eloisa perhaps."

"I know that, Mom, and I don't take it for granted."

"I don't know that I agree with you there. Not that I'm condemning you and your brothers for it. Children should enjoy those traditions and be able to count on them over the years. That gives them roots to ground them when storms hit. Like when your father died. You carried a part of him with you in our traditions."

"What are you trying to say?" He was damn near turning backflips to figure Eloisa out and now his mom was going on about Thanksgiving turkeys and Christmas trees? "Mom, you're talking chick talk, and I'm a guy."

"If you want to keep her, you need to help her feel secure." Ginger released the Stop button and leaned to kiss her son on the cheek. "Now go take care of your wife. I look forward to talking with Eloisa more downstairs whenever the two of you are ready. Your brothers and I will be waiting."

A half hour later, Eloisa waited in the resort lounge with her luggage and Jonah's immense family. She was nervous, even lightly nauseated at this unexpected turn.

She and Jonah had barely had time to talk when he returned from the elevator. He'd simply apologized for his family's surprise intrusion and promised to get her to Audrey before her sister returned from Vegas. He would take care of everything, he'd assured her, giving her a quick but intense kiss before escorting her downstairs.

Fresh paint—mustard yellow—tinted the air and soured her stomach even more. Being with Jonah offered a world of excitement, but very few moments of peace, in spite of the panoramic setting.

Archways framed the two massive walls of windows showcasing the canyon. Stars twinkled in the night sky, the moon climbing. He'd promised they would still leave for Pensacola this evening. He vowed he understood her need to check on Audrey, even if his eyes seemed to say he thought she was overreacting.

Meanwhile, she was stuck in the middle of a very bizarre family reunion. She forced herself not to fidget in the mammoth tapestry wingback. He promised only his mother and lawyer brother knew the truth about their marriage and her family. Apparently the other brothers just thought she was a girlfriend. Having people learn the truth about her background scared Eloisa to the roots of her hair—but at least she didn't have to deal with everyone knowing.

Yet.

She stared at all four Landis men sprawled on red leather sofas, the only pieces of furniture, other than her chair, not wrapped in warehouse plastic. All four men shared the same blue eyes as their mother. Their hair was varying shades of brown. Jonah's was longer.

But there was no mistaking the strong family jaw. These were powerful men, most likely stubborn men. She suspected they got it from their mom.

Ginger Landis Renshaw paced on the lanai, taking a work call, her shoulder-length grey-blond hair perfectly styled. Eloisa recalled from news reports the woman was in her early fifties, but she carried the years well. Wearing a lilac lightweight sweater set with pearls—and blue jeans—Ginger Landis wasn't at all what Eloisa had expected. Thank goodness, because the woman she'd met appeared a little less intimidating.

She'd seen Ginger on the news often enough, reminding Eloisa that she'd followed press coverage of the Landis family all year with more than casual interest. From her attention to the news blogs and video snippets on television, Eloisa knew Ginger was poised and intelligent, sometimes steely determined. Today, a softer side showed as she glanced through the window at her son then over to Eloisa before she returned her attention to her business call.

The whole group was beyond handsome, their unity, happiness and deep sense of connectedness tangible even through the airwaves. And yes, she'd been searching for even a glimpse of Jonah in those photos and broadcasts all year long, too.

How had his mother managed to build such a cohesive family? She searched Ginger's every move through the glass as if somehow she could figure out the answer like a subject researched deeply enough in her library. Then one of his brothers stepped in front of the window, blocking her view. She searched her memory for which brother...

The oldest, Matthew Landis, was a South Carolina senator and the consummate charming politician. "Our baby brother, Jonah, here has always been good at playing things low-key, keeping a lookout in such a way nobody even knew you were watching, but even we didn't see this one coming." Matthew turned to Jonah. "Where have you been hiding this lovely woman?"

Jonah reached from the sofa to rest a hand on her arm. "We met in Spain last summer."

He kept it simple, uncomplicated. How surreal to sit here so casually in this serene retreat while her world exploded around her.

Audrey's life in upheaval.

Secrets with Jonah so close to exposure.

Nowhere to hide from the fact that she was falling hard for Jonah Landis.

She folded her shaking hands in her lap and kept up the pretense of calm conversation. If nothing else, she had a brief window with his brothers before they saw her differently. She could use this chance to learn more about Jonah—from someone else this time. "He kept the lookout how?"

Jonah interjected. "Let's not go there right now."

Kyle grinned. "Let's do. The odds are three to one in our favor, bro."

The world of brothers was fairly alien to her, other than a few brief days nearly twenty years ago.

Sebastian—the lawyer—stretched his arms along the

back of the sofa. "He kept Mom from discovering our tunnels."

"Tunnels?"

Kyle—the brother who'd served in the military—leaned forward, elbows on his knees. "When Sebastian, Jonah and I were kids, during summer vacation, we would pack up sandwiches and Kool-Aid and head out for the day."

"You played at the beach alone?" She glanced out at Ginger and couldn't imagine her tolerating that.

"Nope," Kyle continued, "we went into the more-wooded areas nearby. Sebastian and I dug underground tunnels. Jonah stood guard and warned us if any adults came near."

Sebastian's solemn expression lightened. "We would dig the trench, lay boards over the trough and cover the planks with dirt."

"What about your oldest brother?" She nodded toward Matthew.

Kyle elbowed the esteemed senator. "Too much of a rule follower. He wasn't invited. Although I guess our secret is out now."

"Secret?" Matthew extended his legs in front of him. "Did it ever occur to you to wonder why those tunnels never collapsed on top of you?"

Scowling, Kyle straightened indignantly. "We built damn good tunnels."

"Okay." Matthew spread his hands. "If that's what you want to believe."

"It's what happened." Kyle frowned. "Isn't it?"

The more contemplative Sebastian even shifted uncomfortably until Matthew shook his head, laughing.

"After you two went inside, Jonah would go back out and fix your tunnels. He had me stand guard."

The stunned looks on Sebastian and Kyle's faces were priceless.

Matthew continued, "He was an architect in the making, even then."

Brow furrowing suspiciously, Kyle scrubbed his jaw. "You're yanking our chain."

Sebastian said, "You two collaborated against us?"

"We collaborated *for* you. And if you hadn't excluded us from hanging out in your tunnels we probably would have showed you how to dig them right in the first place rather than laughing at you behind your back."

Kyle slugged his brother on the arm, which started a free-for-all of laughter and light payback punches between the siblings. Did her Medina brothers share moments and memories like this? Did she have the courage to find out? They had no real connection to her other than blood.

But her sister, Audrey? They may not have had the perfect family circle like the Landises, but she loved her sister and her sister loved her. She had to be there for her.

As Jonah had been there for his brothers all those years ago, protecting their secret while making sure they stayed safe. Even as a little kid, the youngest of the crew, he'd been a guardian, a protector, all things that made her fall even harder for him now.

Her throat clogged with emotion and tears, and God, she didn't know how much more enlightenment she could take in one day. Her emotions were already so raw.

And scary.

She turned to Jonah, caught his attention and lightly touched her watch. *We need to leave,* she said with her eyes.

For more reasons than just Audrey. She needed distance to think, because sitting here with the Landises, she wanted to be a part of Jonah's world so much it hurt. This wasn't a family who ran from responsibilities or commitments. *Jonah* was a man to depend on.

And right now, she wasn't so sure she was the kind of woman he deserved.

The next morning, Eloisa propped her elbows on her kitchen island, a mug of tea in her hands as she sat on a barstool next to her sister. Her *married* sister.

A thin silver band glinted on Audrey's finger.

Eloisa and Jonah had taken a red-eye flight back, arriving just at sunrise. She'd hoped they could talk on the plane but he'd received a call from the Peru developers who were working round the clock on plans for the project he would tackle after leaving here.

Leaving her.

After they'd landed, she'd been stunned to find her sister waiting at the town house. With Joey who now stood out on the patio with Jonah.

Eloisa covered her sister's hand. "I'm sorry I wasn't here for you when you needed me."

"I'm an adult, in spite of what our father thinks. I made this decision on my own." Her mouth pinched tight. "Joey wanted to elope and leave this town from the start. I never should have let Dad talk me into a big wedding."

"Don't be too hard on yourself. We want the people we love to be happy."

Audrey looked out the patio doors. "I really shouldn't be so tough on Dad. I was as guilty as him, being charmed by all the money. Dad was always so freaked out about having enough for Mom. I remember this one time he bought her a diamond-and-sapphire necklace. She loved it, but the whole time Dad kept apologizing that it wasn't bigger. He said he wanted her to feel like a queen."

A queen? Had her father known more than she realized? If so, this was rapidly turning into the worst-kept secret on the planet. "Mom loved him."

"I know. I want that for my own marriage." She clasped both her sister's hands, her whisper-pale hair falling to mix with Eloisa's jet black. "It just took me a while to realize it's not about the trappings. I know you probably think I'm crazy for running off."

She thought of her own elopement a year ago. It had seemed so right at the time, she could relate to how her sister felt. Guilt pinched at a corner of her heart. Maybe if she hadn't kept it secret all year long, Audrey might have been encouraged to make her decision earlier. "I may understand better than you think."

She looked out to the patio where Jonah and Joey chatted like old buds. How easily Jonah talked to people, how quick he was to put Joey at ease. Jonah might not embrace the public eye as much as his famous family, but he'd certainly inherited a winning way with people. He'd certainly won *her* over a year ago—and last night. He'd slid under her boundaries in a way no man ever had.

Audrey gazed out at Joey with a seriously love-sick look in her eyes. "I only wish I'd followed my instincts earlier. It would have saved you so much work and time."

Her sister appeared amazingly calm. It seemed all the drama had come from Harry.

Eloisa sipped her tea while her sister shared details about her hurried wedding in a Vegas chapel. "And Joey says we really can't build a life for ourselves here. His family would be involved in anything we try." She took a bracing breath. "So we're relocating. We don't know where yet. He says that's part of the adventure, figuring out where. Maybe we'll toss a dart at a map."

Audrey was embracing the same kind of future Eloisa could have with Jonah. Was that why her sister's words sent a bolt of envy through her? Not that she wasn't happy for Audrey, because this would be a wise move for her. But it would be difficult to see Audrey living the dreams Eloisa had walked away from.

Her eyes tracked back to Jonah again, his broad shoulders, his comfort in watching out for other people, whether it was his older brothers or her. She wanted this happiness for herself, too. She wanted to trust they could work out a way for her to fit her life with his.

She wanted to find the same surety she saw shining from Audrey. There was a vibrancy and strength of purpose in her sister that hadn't been there before. Audrey had gone from pale and ethereal to glittering like a diamond.

"You're really excited about the new adventure."

Ashley clutched Eloisa's hands. "Is that too selfish of me? You've always been here for me and now I'm leaving you."

A deeper truth, an understanding resonated inside her. "You're living your own life. You deserve that. We won't stop being sisters just because you're married, even if you live clear across country. I'll come see you. Pick somewhere interesting, okay?"

Audrey nodded, tears in her eyes as she opened her arms. Eloisa gathered her sister close, hope for her own future glinting ever so warily inside her.

Jonah pushed open the French doors to the patio, his shoulders, his unmistakable charisma filling the void, filling her. She looked into those clear blue eyes of his and knew in her heart. He wasn't out for revenge. He was here for her.

He'd stood by her today during a family crisis. Had intervened for her during her sister's awkward engagement party, had hidden their secret from most of his family. He was a great guy and she trusted him enough to take the next step. She didn't want him to leave for Peru. She wanted longer to test out what they had before it was too late. She deserved a future of her own with Jonah, and the time had come to claim it, obstacles and all.

Starting with telling him about their baby.

Thirteen

Eloisa closed the town house door after Audrey and Joey. Their laughter and playfulness out in the parking lot drifted through, teasing and tempting her with what a relationship could be.

Jonah walked up behind her, swept aside her hair and pressed his mouth to the sensitive curve of her neck. Her head fell back to give him better access. After the day they'd had, there was nothing she wanted more than to lose herself in the forgetfulness reliably found in his arms. Then she could curl up beside him and sleep like a regular married couple.

Except that would be hiding. That would be using sex to shield herself from making the tough step of opening herself totally to Jonah. Letting herself love him.

And even scarier, letting him love her.

She was actually pretty good at loving other people.

Not so good at letting them be there for her. And wasn't that a mind-blowing revelation she would have liked the time to mull over? Except she was out of time.

Deciding to do something and actually following through were two different matters. But she was determined to see this through before they landed in bed.

Eloisa stroked along the open collar of his simple button-down, wishing her nerves were as easily smoothed. "Thank you for being so understanding about coming back here for Audrey. I hated cutting short your visit with your family."

"They're the ones who showed up unannounced." He looped his hands low around her waist. "We can have more time with them soon if you want."

"I do."

His face kicked up in a one-sided smile. "Good, good."

Jonah tucked her against his side and strode deeper into the living area, out to the patio. He drew her down with him in the Adirondack chair, settling her in his lap with such an ease and rightness it took her breath away. How could such a big-boned, hard-bodied man make for such a comfortable resting spot?

Eloisa nestled her head on his shoulder and gazed outward. That would be easier than looking him in the face. The sky turned hazy shades of purple and grey as the sun surrendered and night muscled upward.

Jonah thumbed along the back of her neck, massaging tiny kinks. "I'm sorry for not taking into account your job, and your need for security. I can understand why following me from job to job may not sound like the best of lives for you. We'll work together to figure out a solution."

God, he made it sound possible to find a compromise. She wanted to trust it could be that simple.

"Is that what we're talking about?" She swallowed hard against the hope. "A life together?"

"I think we're most definitely moving in that direction." His chin rested on top of her head. "It would be a mistake to pretend otherwise."

"Okay then—" she inhaled a shaky breath, not nearly bolstering enough "—if we're being totally honest here, there's something I need to tell you, something that will be difficult to say and difficult to hear."

His arms stiffened around her, but he kept his chin resting in her hair. "Are you walking out again?"

"No, not unless you tell me to." Which could very well happen. A trickle of fear iced up her spine. What if she'd put this off until too late? Would he understand her reasons for waiting?

"That'll never happen."

"You sound so sure." She wanted to be as certain. But hadn't being with Jonah helped her see she couldn't plan for everything? "You're always full of absolutes, total confidence."

"I have a vision for our future and it's perfect." He tipped her face up to his. "You're perfect. We're going to be perfect together."

"You can't really believe I'm perfect. And if you think that even on some level, what are you going to do when my many flaws show?" Of course she was afraid of rejection after a lifetime of being shuffled aside through no fault of her own. A child didn't deserve that. Except now, she was an adult and had no one to blame but herself. "What if I don't fit into the beautiful world of no boundaries that you've engineered for yourself?"

"We'll work at it. Think about your graduate studies in Spain. You enjoyed your research contribution. Maybe that's a path to blending our worlds again. Or we split time, both making compromises."

He was offering her so much that she wasn't prepared to think about yet. Not until she'd taken care of this old hurt. "That's not what I'm talking about. It's something different, something bigger, a mistake I made."

He stroked her forehead. "You're such a serious person, and while I admire the way you care about the feelings of everyone around you, I'm a big boy. Now just cut to the chase and say it."

"I haven't been completely honest with you—" her heart pounded so hard her ribs hurt "—about more than just my father."

"Do you have a boyfriend on the side?"

"Good Lord, Jonah—" her hands fisted in his shirt "—I've spent the whole year aching for you. There's no room for anyone else."

"Then no worries." He winked.

Winked, damn it.

"Jonah, please don't joke. Not now. This is difficult enough as it is." She pushed the words up and out as fast as she could. "After we split up, after I left you, I found out I was pregnant with your child."

His hold on her loosened, his face swiped free of any expression. "You had a baby," he said slowly, his voice flat, neutral. "Our baby."

She nodded, her heart hammering all the harder through pools of tears bottled inside. The grief, the loneliness and regret splashed through her again with each thud of her pulse. She should have called him then. But she hadn't and now it was time to face the consequences for that decision. "I had a miscarriage."

"When?"

"Does it even matter?" She hated the way her voice hitched.

"I deserve to know when...how long."

She flinched with guilt. He was right. He deserved that and so much more. "I miscarried at four and a half months. Nobody knew except my doctor and my priest."

She wanted him to know that while she hadn't told him, she'd nurtured and honored that life even if he hadn't been there to witness it. Even if he was going to walk out, he deserved to know that.

The first shadows of emotion chased across his face—incredulity. "You didn't even tell your sister?"

"Audrey had just gotten engaged to Joey," she rushed to explain, and it sounded so lame now but had made such sense then. "I didn't want to spoil her special time."

"No," he said simply, his body shifting, tensing, no longer the welcoming place to land. Something had unmistakably changed between them. "I'm not buying the excuses."

She agreed, but still she'd hoped for some... understanding? Sympathy? Comfort after the fact? "What? I tell you my most heartbreaking secret and you just say 'no.' What's the matter with you?"

She couldn't bear to sit in his arms that had become so stone-cold. She rolled to her feet and backed away.

He stood slowly, his hands in his pockets. No warm reception for her revelation. "I think you didn't tell your sister because then you'd have to let someone get close to you, be a part of your life. Don't you think she would be hurt to know you didn't feel like you could turn to her?"

She hadn't thought of it that way before and she didn't know what to make of the notion now. Her confessions had churned up the loss for her, the retelling of it bringing to mind those dark hours when the blood loss started, then being in the hospital alone. The grief when the doctor told her the baby's heartbeat had stopped. The teeth-chattering cold after her D and C.

Would having her sister there have made the pain go away? Right now, with the memories fresh in her mind, she couldn't think of anything that would ease the loss for her.

And oh God, why hadn't she given more thought to how this would hurt Jonah? She forced herself to look in his eyes and confront the pain—and yes, the anger—she found there. "I should have told you then."

"Damn straight, you should have," he snapped, the anger seeping into his voice as well. "But you didn't. Because that would involve me being a part of your life and your family when it's easier to hide in your library with your books."

She gasped at the stab of his words. "You're being cruel."

"I'm being realistic for the first time, Eloisa." He paced the small stone patio restlessly, the frustration in his tone building with every step. "You talk about wanting a future together but you've been keeping this from me the whole time, even when we made love."

"I'm telling you the truth now. Just five minutes ago you said nothing could break us apart."

"Would you have told me if you weren't afraid I would find out anyway, now that all your secrets are coming out?" He pivoted back sharply to face her, the moonlight casting harsh shadows down his angry face. "When have you ever willingly let me into your life?"

She couldn't think of an answer. He'd led their relationship every step of the way.

He started toward her again. "All this time I've been wondering if you can trust me, and now I don't know if I can trust you. I don't know if I can be with you, always wondering when you're going to run again." He stopped pacing abruptly and plowed his hand through his hair. "This is too much. I can't wrap my brain around it. I need air."

He jammed his hands into his pockets again as if he couldn't even bear to touch her and left. The front door closed quietly but firmly behind him.

The first tear slipped free and pulled the plug out of the dam for the rest to come flooding down. Barely able to see, she walked back into her town house.

For the past year, she'd been immersed in her own pain and fears, never once thinking about how much she must have hurt Jonah when she'd left him. Now, standing alone with the echo of that lone door click in her ears, in her soul, she realized just how fully she'd screwed up in leaving him.

She was totally alone for the first time in her life. Harry was upset she hadn't persuaded Audrey to stay. Audrey was off enjoying marital bliss. And Jonah had left her. She had nowhere to turn.

Eloisa stood in the middle of her empty town house that had once felt like a haven and now seemed so very barren. She searched for something, any piece of comfort. Her fingers trailed over the glass paperweight, the one she'd made from shells and a dried flower, memorializing her baby's too-brief life. What would it have been like to share that grief with Jonah?

And now because of how she'd handled things, he was suffering the loss alone as well.

She gripped the cool paperweight in her hand—and revealed a plain white card with ten typed numbers, Duarte's number.

Perhaps there was at least one thing she could fix in her messed-up life after all. Perhaps she might as well make someone happy.

Jonah was going to get seriously trashed if his brothers didn't stop pouring drinks for him. But then that's why he'd come home to Hilton Head to be with his family.

Sitting on the balcony at the Landis beachside compound, he nudged away the latest shot glass on the iron outdoor table. He was still reeling from Eloisa's revelation about getting pregnant and losing their baby. Never once bothering to contact him about something so monumental.

Anger still chewed at his gut, along with grief for the child that could have been. And having a child with Eloisa? Even the possibility had his hands shaking so hard he couldn't have picked up the shot glass even if he'd wanted.

As much as he regretted not knowing about the life that had begun inside her a year ago, the knowledge of what happened made him realize the importance of getting things right with Eloisa this time. If birth control had failed a year ago, then it could fail again. He would not risk being on the other side of an ocean if Eloisa carried his child.

After their fight, he'd driven along the beach for about an hour until he'd calmed down enough to talk to her again. He hadn't known what he would say or how they could work through it. His ability to trust her had taken a serious blow. But he was willing to try.

Except once he returned to her town house, he found she'd already left. Her car was gone. Her suitcase was gone. Eloisa had run away again. Jonah had hopped the first plane to the only place he could think of to go. Home to hang out with his brothers.

Sebastian clanked down his crystal glass, the ocean wind kicking in off the waves. The surf crashed. Sailboat lines pinged against the double mast of the family yacht. "You have to figure out what speaks to her."

Frowning, Kyle leaned toward his brother with an almost imperceptible sway. "Marianna made you go to some kind of woo-woo, Zen-like couples retreat, didn't she?"

Sebastian reached for the bottle of vintage bourbon in the middle of the table. "What makes you say that?"

"'Figure out what speaks to her,'" Kyle mimicked in a spacey-sounding voice before laughing. "Really, dude, who are you and what have you done with my brother?"

Matthew clapped Kyle on the shoulder, the salty breeze filling their shirts, hinting at an incoming storm. "Don't knock it 'til you've tried it. There's something to be said for learning to speak their language on occasion. The benefits are amazing."

Sebastian smiled knowingly.

Jonah turned the glass around and around on the

table, a tic starting in the corner of his eye. He wondered for the first time how all his Neanderthal brothers had managed to find great women. What did they know that he didn't? What was he missing?

Hunger for making things work with Eloisa compelled him to flat-out ask. He sure as hell wasn't making headway alone. "You're going to have to 'speak' to me in regular-guy English if you expect me to understand."

Sebastian's face took on the lawyer look he assumed right before rolling out his best case. Of course the look was a little deflated by his cockeyed tie. "Okay, standard red roses and a heart-shaped box of chocolates are all well and good, and certainly better than not doing anything. But if you can think of something personal, something that says you know her...you'll be golden."

Kyle scratched the back of his head, his hair still worn short even after he'd finished his military commitment. "They really like to know we're thinking about them when they're not around."

Jonah eyed his brothers in disbelief. God, they were making his head hurt worse rather than helping. "Do you all get a group discount for the couples retreat?"

"Bro, make fun all you want," Matthew said. "You can have our advice or flounder around on your own."

"It's actually not that complicated," Sebastian explained. "Marianna adores our dogs." They both were nuts over their two mutts, Buddy and Holly. "One Valentine's Day, I bought Coach collars and leashes for the dogs, along with a donation to the local Humane Society."

Kyle jabbed a finger in his direction. "Remember when I got the laptop computer for Phoebe? Her squeal of excitement just about rattled every window."

Hearing how his brothers hit just the perfect note to make their wives happy offered up a special torture for him now that Eloisa had damn near ripped his heart out. "You had me tuck the wrapped computer where she would see it while you took her on a date."

Kyle smiled, his eyes taking on a distant air. "A late-night drive in a vintage Aston Martin convertible."

"Wow!" Matthew whistled low. "Nice move."

"Thanks." Kyle refilled his glass. "I'll give you the name of the guy who hooked me up. Now back to the computer." He turned toward Jonah, porch lights the only illumination, with the clouds covering the stars. "Phoebe was stretched too thin teaching her online classes and caring for the baby. I offered to take time off from work to watch Nina, even offered more nanny time, but she wasn't budging. The laptop gave her a way of working from anywhere."

His brother had done a damn fine job at blending two diverse lifestyles. Kyle and Phoebe might well have some good advice for Eloisa...if he hadn't walked out on her. If she hadn't followed up by walking out on him again as well.

It downright sucked being around these guys who practically oozed satisfaction and marital bliss.

Matthew snagged the bottle from his brother. "Extravagant is cool, too, you've just got to mix it up some with the practical."

Clinking the ice, Kyle lifted his glass for a refill. "What's Ashley's extravagance?"

Matthew's mouth twitched with a hint of a smile. "Don't think I can share that with you, my brother."

"Hey." Kyle raised his hands. "Fair enough."

The sound of a throat clearing reverberated behind them. They all four twisted in their seats.

Their mother's second husband—General Hank Renshaw—stood in the open French doors. His distinguished military bearing was still visible even after his retirement. His hair might be solid gray now, but he had a sharp brain that made him a major player in the national defense arena. "Hope you boys have saved at least one drink of my best alcohol for me."

"Yes, sir." Kyle snagged another glass from the tray they'd brought out with them and passed their stepfather—a lifetime family friend as well—a drink. "Maybe you can help Jonah here figure out how to get his wife back."

"Hmmm..." The General tipped back his glass with only a slight wince and dragged a chair over to the table. "Well, your mother likes it when I—"

"Whoa! Whoa! Hold on there a minute, General." The protests of all four brothers tumbled over each other.

Jonah agreed one hundred percent on that staying a secret. "That's our mom you're talking about. While I appreciate the offer to help, there are just some things a son doesn't need to know."

Matthew drained his glass. "The time we walked in on the two of you damn near gave me a heart attack."

"Okay, okay." The General chuckled lowly. "I get the picture." His laughter faded and he jabbed a thumb toward the door. "Now how about you three take the bottle and clear out so I can talk to Jonah?"

Chairs scraped back and his brothers abandoned ship. The slugging and laughs faded in the hall and up the stairs.

The General refilled both glasses. "Your dad was my best friend." He lifted his in toast. "He would be proud of you."

"Thank you. That means a lot to me." But not enough to clear away the frustration over failing when it counted most.

With Eloisa.

Why had she kept the news from him then? And now? He needed to understand that if they stood a chance at stopping this cycle of turning each other inside out, then running for opposite corners.

He didn't expect the General was going to be able to offer some magic bullet to fix everything any more than his brothers had. But still he appreciated the support. The General had been there for them after their dad died. He'd always vowed he was just helping out their mom the way she'd helped him after his wife died. But they'd all wondered how long it would take....

"It takes as long as it takes. But you don't quit."

How had the General known what he was thinking? "Have you added a mind reader medal to your already impressive collection?"

"Quit beating yourself up about the past and move forward," the General said with clipped, military efficiency. "Don't just curl up and admit defeat. You've got an opportunity now. Run with it."

"She's gone." Jonah reached into his pocket and pulled out the white card he'd found by her telephone, the same card he remembered Duarte Medina giving her. He flipped the number between his fingers. "She doesn't want to speak to me or see me again."

"And you're going to just quit? Give up on your marriage? Give up on her?"

His fingers slowed, the numbers on the vellum square coming into focus. His whole life coming into focus as well, because this time he wasn't letting Eloisa just walk away. There was a way to break this cycle after all. Show her how a real family came through for each other, everyone offering support rather than the one-sided deal she'd lived, always being the one giving. No wonder she hadn't reached out to him when she was hurting.

No one had ever given her reason to think her call for help would be answered.

This time he intended to show her that somebody loved her—*he* loved her—enough to follow and stay. "You have a point, General." He tapped the simple white card. "Lucky for me, I think I know exactly how to find her."

Fourteen

Eloisa sat on her father's garden patio overlooking the Atlantic, waiting. In minutes she would see Enrique Medina again. How surreal and confusing, and so not the joyful reunion she'd dreamed of as a child.

She turned to Duarte standing beside her somberly. "Thank you for arranging this meeting so quickly."

"Don't thank me," he answered with no warmth. "If it were up to me, we would all go about our lives separately. But this is how he wants it and, bottom line, it's his call to make."

His brusqueness made her edgier, as if she wasn't already about to jump out of her skin. She searched for something benign to diffuse the tension. "The rocky shoreline looks exactly like the one I remember from that single visit—magnificent. I often wondered if my memory was faulty."

"Apparently not."

And apparently Duarte would need more prodding to speak. "How strange to think our father has been so close all this time? In the same state even?"

Her biological father had taken up residence on a small private island off the coast of St. Augustine, Florida. One call to Duarte had set everything in motion. Her heart bruised beyond bearing, she'd been on a private jet, flying away from Jonah and the catastrophic mess she'd made of their second chance. Her throat clogged with more tears. She swallowed them and narrowed her attention to satisfying her curiosity about this place she'd thought of so often.

The towering white stucco house, rustling palm trees, massive archways and crashing waves... She could have been seven again, with her mother beside her, waiting for *him* to greet them.

Duarte touched her arm lightly, bringing her back to the moment. "Eloisa? He's here."

The lanai doors creaked opened. But no imposing king stepped out this time. An electric wheelchair hummed the only warning before Enrique came outside. Two large, lopey dogs followed in perfect sync. Confined to the chair, he was thin, gray and weary.

Duarte hadn't lied. Their father appeared near death. She stood but didn't reach out. A hug would have seemed strange, affected. The emotion forced. She didn't know what she felt for him. He'd needed her and beckoned. It was difficult not to resent all the times she'd needed him. Yes, he'd made contact through his lawyer over the years, but so infrequently and impersonally it seemed she was merely an afterthought. Her mind jetted back to that strange, but endearing, Landis family gathering at

Jonah's elegant Texas resort. This family reunion bore no resemblance to that one.

"Hello, sir. You'll have to pardon me if I'm not quite sure what to call you."

He waved dismissively, perspiration dotting his forehead. "Call me Enrique." His body might be weak, but his voice still commanded attention. The Spanish accent was almost as thick as she remembered. "I do not want formality or deserve any titles, king or father. Now sit down, please. I feel like a rude old man for not standing with a lovely lady present."

She took her seat again and he whirred the chair into position in front of her. The two brown dogs—Ridgebacks, perhaps?—settled on either side. He studied her silently, his hands folded in his lap, veins bruised from what appeared to be frequent IV needles.

Still, no matter the sallow pallor and thinner frame, Enrique Medina's face was that of royalty. His aristocratic nose and chiseled jaw spoke of his age-old warrior heritage. There was strength in that face, despite everything. And while his heavy blue robe with emerald-green silk lapels was not the garb of a king in his prime, the rich fabrics and sleek leather slippers reflected his wealth.

The old king gestured toward the doors. "Duarte, you can leave us now. I have some things to say to Eloisa alone."

Duarte nodded, turning away without a word, walking off with steps quieter than those of anyone she'd known. But he wasn't her reason for being here today. She'd come to see her father, to hopefully find some peace and resolution inside herself.

"I'm sorry you're ill."

"So am I."

He didn't speak further, and she wondered if perhaps he'd started to lose his mental faculties. She glanced up at the male nurse waiting patiently at the doorway. No answers there.

She looked back at Enrique. "You asked to see me? You sent Duarte."

"Of course I did. I'm not losing my mind yet anyway." He straightened his lapels. "Please forgive me for being rude. I was merely struck by how much you resemble my mother. She was quite lovely, too."

"Thank you." It would have been nice to have met her grandmother or even see pictures like other kids growing up. Maybe it wasn't too late. "Do you have photos of her?"

"They were all lost when my home was burned to the ground."

She blinked fast. Not the answer she'd expected. She'd read what little was reported on the coup in San Rinaldo twenty-seven years ago. She knew her father had barely escaped with his life—his wife had not. He and his sons had gone into hiding. And while she understood the danger, she'd never truly thought of all he'd lost.

Certainly losing a picture wasn't the same as losing a person, but to have lost even those bits of comfort and reminders... "Then we'll have to make sure you have a picture of me to remember her by."

"Thank you, but I imagine I will be seeing her soon enough." He spoke of his death so matter-of-factly it stunned her. "Which brings me to why I called for you, *pequeña princesa*."

Little princess? Small princess? Either way, she'd never dared think of herself with that title. More than anything, her heart stumbled on the endearment that Harry had always applied to his biological daughter and never to her. Not that she would let mere words sway her after all this time.

Enrique steadied his breathing. "There are some things you need to know and time is short. Whether I die or someone finally finds me, our secret will come out someday. Even I can only hold back that tide for just so long."

The thought of that kind of exposure sent her reaching for the lemonade beside her. What if the king's enemies sought him out again? Sought her out? "Where will you hide then?"

If he was still alive.

"I am a king." His chin tipped. "I do not hide. I stay here for the people I love."

"I'm not sure I follow what you mean."

"By staying here, it keeps up the illusion that I—and my children—are in Argentina. No one bothers to look for them. No one can hurt them the way they went after my Beatriz."

Beatriz, his wife who'd been gunned down during the escape. "That must have been awful for you."

And her brothers.

His chin tipped higher as he looked away for a moment unblinking. Seeing the Herculean strength of will in a man so weak...

He focused his intense dark eyes on her again. "It was difficult meeting your mother so soon after my Beatriz was murdered. I did love your mother, as much as I could at that time. She told me if she could not have my full heart, she wanted nothing."

She'd always thought her mother stayed away because

of safety reasons. She'd never considered her mom acted out of emotion. Harry Taylor may not be anyone's idea of Prince Charming, but he had adored her mother. Eloisa sat back in her chair and let Enrique talk. He seemed to need to unload burdens. For the first time, she realized how much she needed to listen.

"I am sorry I did not get to watch you grow up. Nothing I can do now will make up for the fact I was not the father you deserved."

The humble honesty of that simple statement meant more to her than any amount of money. She'd been waiting a lifetime to hear him admit he should have been a father to her.

And while that didn't erase the past, it was a first step toward a healing. She brushed her fingers over his bruised hand, words escaping her.

"I did decide to ask your mother to marry me."

"What happened?"

"I finally looked past my grief to see a new chance at love waiting."

"She didn't want to live here?"

"Oh no, she wouldn't have minded staying here. She told me so. I just waited too long to ask."

Oh my God. "She'd already married Harry."

"I fought for her six months too late," he said simply. "Don't wait too long to fight, *pequeña princesa*."

But her chance was gone now.

This time, Jonah had left her. She wanted to shout her hurt and pain over the way he'd left, even knowing she'd brought it on herself. He was the one who'd walked out, not her. Enrique didn't understand. How could he? He didn't know her. He couldn't, not from detective reports or however he'd kept watch over her life.

She started to tell him just that but something in his eyes stopped her, a deep wisdom that came from experiences she couldn't begin to comprehend. This man knew what it meant to fight.

And his blood ran through her veins.

Eloisa gripped the arms of her chair with a newfound strength. She was through hiding in her library and in her fears. She loved Jonah Landis and wanted a life with him, wherever that life took them. He was hurting and angry now, and she couldn't blame him. She hadn't put her heart on the line for him. Taking cautious to a new level. But she would remedy that now. She was in this for the long haul.

She would fight for him so damn hard he wouldn't know what hit him.

Pushing to her feet, she cupped Enrique's face in her hands. "You certainly are a devious old man, but I do believe I like you."

His laugh rumbled as he gave her a smile and a regal nod.

Eloisa backed away slowly until her hands fell to her sides. "I have to go, but I will come back. I just need to clear up some things with Jonah first."

Her father raised his hand and twirled a finger. "Turn around."

What? Frowning, she glanced over her shoulder. And her heart lodged squarely in her throat.

Jonah stood waiting in the archway, his hair slicked back and flowers in his hand.

Jonah barely had time to nod to Eloisa's father before the old king vacated the porch, leaving him alone with her. He owed Duarte and Enrique for making this reunion happen.

And he intended to repay them by keeping Eloisa safe and happy for the rest of her life.

He closed the last few steps between them, flowers extended. "I don't know what specific kind of gift you would want that 'speaks' to your soul, so I had to settle for flowers. But they're pink tulips, like the picture on your wall. I figured you must have chosen it because you like them."

"They're perfect! Thank you." Taking the flowers in one hand, she pressed her fingers to his lips with her other. The ocean wind molded her sundress to her body just the way it had when he'd seen her again outside her sister's engagement party. They'd covered a lot of ground in a few short days.

"Jonah, I so was wrong when I said we don't know each other." She brought the tulips up just under her nose and inhaled. "The flowers are lovely but you've already given me exactly what speaks to my soul. You give me infinity pools and walk with me through dusty castles full of history. You coax me out of my dark office and you even compliment my apple-flavored lip gloss. You know everything about me except—" she arched up on her toes, the flowers crushed lightly between them "—how very deeply I love you."

He swept her hair back and cradled her head, the subtle scent of tulips mixing with the tangy salt air and the essence of *her*. "I know now—" thank God "—and look forward to telling you and showing you just how much I love you in every country around the world. If you're up for the adventure?"

"I like the sound of those ideas you discussed earlier

for blending our lives together. I think I'm more than ready to bring my library research world out into the field again. As long as you're there with me."

She angled her head to meet his kiss, the taste of apples and the touch of her tongue familiar and far too exciting when they could be interrupted at any second.

"We should speak to your father."

"Soon," she said, her smile fading. "But first I need you to know how sorry I am for not telling you about the baby right when I found out, and then for not telling you once we got involved again. That was wrong of me to keep it from you. You deserved to know."

"Thank you for that. You didn't have to say it, but I appreciate hearing it." The knowledge of that loss still hurt, and he suspected it would for a long time. But he understood how difficult it was for her to trust. He expected he would still have some work to do in easing away barriers she'd spent a lifetime erecting.

But he was damn good at renovations, at making something magnificent from the foundation already in place. "I brought something else for you besides the flowers."

"You didn't have to bring me anything. You're being here means more than I can say."

"I should have followed you before. I should have been there for you."

She cupped his face. "We're moving forward, remember?" Eloisa kissed him again, and once more, holding for three intense heartbeats. "Now what did you want to show me?"

He reached into his pocket and pulled out two gold bands. Theirs. He'd kept them the whole year. Her eyes bright with her smile and unshed tears, she held up her hand. He slid Eloisa's wedding ring onto her finger, and she slid his in place again as well, clasping his hand tightly in hers. This time, he knew, those rings weren't coming off again.

Jonah tugged one of the tulips from the bouquet and tucked it behind her ear. "Are you ready to go inside now, Mrs. Landis?"

She hooked her arm in his, like a bride with her bouquet. "I'm ready to go absolutely anywhere…with *you.*"

Epilogue

Lima, Peru: Two Months Later

She had dreamed she was draped in jewels.

Languishing in twilight slumber, Eloisa Landis skimmed her fingers along the bare arm of the man sleeping next to her. She'd had the sweetest dream that her husband had showered her with emeralds and rubies and fat freshwater pearls while they'd made love. She stroked up Jonah's arms to face, his five-o'clock shadow rasping against her tender fingertips.

Eloisa flipped to her back and stretched, extending her arm so the sun refracted off her cushion-cut diamond ring to go alongside her wedding band. Early morning light streaked through the wrought-iron window grilles in the adobe manor home he'd rented for the summer. A gentle breeze rustled the linen draping over the bed.

What was it about this man that took her breath away?

His hand fell to her hip and she smiled.

Yeah, she knew exactly what drew her to him. Everything.

Growling low, he hauled her against his side. "The rubies, definitely the rubies," he said as he peeked through one eye, apparently not as asleep as she'd imagined. He flicked the dangling gems on her ears. "I've been dreaming of draping you in jewels for over a year."

"You certainly played out that fantasy last night." She reached underneath her to sweep free a sapphire bracelet that was poking into her back.

How delightfully ironic that he was the one giving her jewels and castles. Not that she needed any of it. She had peace and excitement, stability and adventure all at once with the man she loved. "You certainly brought along a king's ransom in jewels."

"Because you're a Landis, lady. That makes you American royalty." He rolled her underneath him, elbows propped.

Royalty. The word didn't make her wince anymore. She was coming to peace with that part of herself. She'd visited her father again. His health was still waning, his liver failing. She would have to face that, no more hiding for her. But thank goodness she had Jonah at her side to deal with the worst when it came around.

Jonah kissed her lightly, comforting, as if he read her thoughts, something he seemed to do more and more often these days.

Audrey and Joey were well on their way to opening a catering business in Maine, of all places. They said they planned to bring a little southern spice into lobster.

Harry planned to join them and manage the books, always looking out for his daughter's financial future.

Eloisa's family was expanding rapidly, with the Landises due in for a long weekend visit. Ginger had mandated they all needed to get to know their new relative better. Eloisa appreciated the overture. How silly to get so excited about being the belle of the ball.

But she couldn't help herself. The Landises had a way of making her feel special and welcome.

A part of their family.

Jonah toyed with the beaded pearls strung through her hair. "Have you given any thought to where you would like to live?"

"I figure when the right restoration project comes around for our home, we'll know it."

He gave her hair a light tug. "Can you narrow that down to a country for me?"

"Nope—" she threaded her fingers through his hair, drawing him down to her "—I'm through limiting my options out of preconceived notions." She nestled her leg more firmly between his, grazing him with the gold-flecked garter belt around her thigh. "Now, it's all about the possibilities."

* * * * *

Don't miss Catherine Mann's August novella
Part of Desire's new continuity miniseries
A SUMMER FOR SCANDAL
On sale August 10, 2010 from Silhouette Desire.

Harlequin offers a romance for every mood!
See below for a sneak peek
from our suspense romance line
Silhouette® Romantic Suspense.
Introducing HER HERO IN HIDING
by New York Times *bestselling author Rachel Lee.*

Kay Young returned to woozy consciousness to find that she was lying on a soft sofa beneath a heap of quilts near a cheerfully burning fire. When she tried to move, however, everything hurt, and she groaned.

At once she heard a sound, then a stranger with a hard, harsh face was squatting beside her. "Shh," he said softly. "You're safe here. I promise."

"I have to go," she said weakly, struggling against pain. "He'll find me. He can't find me."

"Easy, lady," he said quietly. "You're hurt. No one's going to find you here."

"He will," she said desperately, terror clutching at her insides. "He always finds me!"

"Easy," he said again. "There's a blizzard outside. No one's getting here tonight, not even the doctor. I know, because I tried."

"Doctor? I don't need a doctor! I've got to get away."

"There's nowhere to go tonight," he said levelly. "And if I thought you could stand, I'd take you to a window and show you."

But even as she tried once more to pull away the quilts, she remembered something else: this man had been gentle when he'd found her beside the road, even when she had kicked and clawed. He hadn't hurt her.

Terror receded just a bit. She looked at him and detected signs of true concern there.

The terror eased another notch and she let her head sag on the pillow. "He always finds me," she whispered.

"Not here. Not tonight. That much I can guarantee."

Will Kay's mysterious rescuer
protect her from her worst fears?
Find out in HER HERO IN HIDING by
New York Times *bestselling author Rachel Lee.*
Available June 2010, only from
Silhouette® Romantic Suspense.

HARLEQUIN® *Blaze*™

is proud to present

New York Times bestselling author

Vicki Lewis Thompson

with a brand-new trilogy,
SONS OF CHANCE
where three sexy brothers
meet three irresistible women.

Look for the first book
WANTED!

*Available beginning in June 2010
wherever books are sold.*

---

red-hot reads